THE QUEST FOR THE LOST AMBER ROOM

Terry Q. O'Brien

TQOB Publishing

Copyright © 2025 by TQOB Publishing / Terry Q. O'Brien – All rights reserved.

The events depicted in this story are a blend of fiction and nonfiction. While certain events, locations, or situations may be inspired by real occurrences, the characters, incidents, and dialogue are entirely fictitious. Any resemblance to actual persons, living or deceased, places, buildings, or products is purely coincidental. No identification with actual persons or entities is intended or should be inferred.

No part of this publication, The Quest for the Lost Amber Room, may be reproduced, distributed, or transmitted in any form or by any means, including photocopying, recording, or other electronic or mechanical methods, without the prior written permission of the publisher, except as permitted by U.S. copyright law.

For permission requests, contact: TQOB Publishing, Chicago, Illinois.

ISBN (e-book): 979-8-9927093-2-2
ISBN (paperback): 979-8-9927093-1-5
ISBN (hardcover): 979-8-9927093-0-8
Library of Congress Control Number: 2025901680

Cover Art: Robert Jarocki

terryobrien.com

To Ashley and Austin,

For your love, support, and belief in me.

CONTENTS

CHAPTER 1: The World's Fair – Chicago 1893

CHAPTER 2: The PTE Unit Complex

CHAPTER 3: The New Mission

CHAPTER 4: Map One of Two

CHAPTER 5: Travel Plans

CHAPTER 6: Portation Room

CHAPTER 7: East of Munich

CHAPTER 8: Munich to Berlin

CHAPTER 9: Wolfgang Müller

CHAPTER 10: The *Rubáiyát*

CHAPTER 11: Fifty-Second Parallel

CHAPTER 12: The *Titanic*

CHAPTER 13: Preparation

CHAPTER 14: Cargo Hold

CHAPTER 15: Officers' Quarters

CHAPTER 16: Queenstown, Ireland

CHAPTER 17: Embarkation

CHAPTER 18: Exploring the Ship

CHAPTER 19: Day Two

CHAPTER 20: Last Day

CHAPTER 21: Iceberg!

CHAPTER 22: On Guard

CHAPTER 23: Murdoch's Cabin

CHAPTER 24: Promenade Deck

CHAPTER 25: Separated

CHAPTER 26: Abandon Ship

CHAPTER 27: Seven Horns

CHAPTER 28: Lifeboat #7

CHAPTER 29: Composite C-4

CHAPTER 30: The Lonely Ocean

CHAPTER 31: Escape

CHAPTER 32: A Night to Remember

CHAPTER 33: Lanolin

CHAPTER 34: The Old Woman

CHAPTER 35: Lifeboat #3

CHAPTER 36: The *Carpathia*

CHAPTER 37: The Infirmary

CHAPTER 38: Reunion

CHAPTER 39: The *Errant*

CHAPTER 40: The Deal

CHAPTER 41: The Library

CHAPTER FORTY-TWO: Something Wicked

CHAPTER FORTY-THREE: The Map

CHAPTER FORTY-FOUR: Fire Escape

CHAPTER FORTY-FIVE: No Way Out

CHAPTER FORTY-SIX: Diversion

CHAPTER FORTY-SEVEN: Fire!

CHAPTER FORTY-EIGHT: Rooftops

CHAPTER FORTY-NINE: Trapped

CHAPTER FIFTY: Return Home

EPILOGUE: The Amber Room

Chapter 1
The World's Fair – Chicago, 1893

The three time travelers walked inconspicuously through the White City during the 1893 World's Columbian Exposition. Dressed in period clothing, each wearing dark bowler hats, the three walked through the lavish fairgrounds of the Gilded Age. Chicago had experienced rapid growth in economics, construction, and urban expansion following the Great Chicago Fire of 1871 and the fair welcomed millions from all over the world. Being anonymous was easy, and while touring the vast exposition, the travelers remained virtually unnoticed by the many visitors.

Experienced in avoiding interfering with or changing the past, the time travelers were also well acquainted with the historical details of the 1893 World's Fair. They engaged in only casual conversations that were forgettable and nonconfrontational, as such superficial interactions with attendees did not cause changes in the recorded history. Yet the three knew history was irreversible, and any attempts to alter the past were met with disastrous consequences. The World's Fair would remain as it had been written and locked in time.

Nevertheless, taking a few moments to enjoy the magnificent fair was still breathtaking. At least for Miles Gallagher, the shortest man of the three travelers. As the three passed the Great Basin pond, Gallagher stopped to look at a large statue rising above the water. He marveled in amazement, gazing upon the beauty of the statue. Known as the Statue of the Republic, the grand bronze sculpture featured a robed female figure, one hand grasping a staff and the other supporting an eagle.

Michael Brett walked up next to Gallagher. Brett was taller and strikingly more muscular than Gallagher. "Incredible, isn't it," Brett said, adjusting his bowler hat as he gazed upon the statue.

Before Gallagher could answer, Robert Paulson, the lead traveler for the mission, approached them from behind. He maintained a stoic, focused look on his face. As the craftiest of the three, Paulson was a stealth planner. "Come on. We're not here to sightsee." Paulson nodded toward a building across the pond and began walking. Gallagher, momentarily embarrassed, followed Paulson, while Brett trailed behind.

Their mission was to obtain a Japanese jade necklace from the World's Fair. Designed with five hand-carved pieces around a gold band, the necklace featured an image of a Japanese empress in the center, with two concubines joining her on each side. History recorded the valuable artifact as missing from the Japanese Room on the second floor of the Fine Arts Palace the morning after the travelers' visit to the fair.

The necklace was never recovered, and its whereabouts remained unknown. Rumors circulated about its disappearance, suggesting that someone had accidentally damaged the necklace and hidden their mistake by disposing of the artifact. Paulson believed that a custodian broke and discarded the item to avoid being fired from his job.

Although there was a risk, by successfully removing the necklace before it was lost, the travelers could safely return the artifact to the present without altering the course of the past. Paulson was also acutely aware of the need for a successful outcome, following a series of failed missions. He knew returning the jade necklace to the present day would be met with praise and approval. The odds were in their favor, and Paulson and his fellow time travelers were confident they could extract the jade necklace without detection or de-existence.

After considering the options on how best to retrieve the necklace, Paulson decided the team would break into the Fine Arts Palace after closing hours and steal it then. Passing the Great Basin, the three walked to the base of steps in front of the Fine Arts Palace. Gallagher noticed the two prominent lion statues guarding the outside entrance to the exhibit hall. Looking past them, he saw that Roman pillars supported the ornate building, where tall wooden doors were open, welcoming guests to the exhibit hall. He recognized the building from his own time.

"I can see parts of the Museum of Science and Industry," Gallagher said, referring to the present-day Chicago museum. "The building is one of the few things that remains from the World's Fair."

Brett, who had been walking with his head down, glanced upward. Noticing the large statue, he asked, "Is that statue still at the museum in the future?"

"No," Gallagher responded, referencing his pre-mission research.

Paulson looked up the steps to the twenty-foot doors that led into the exhibition. "Let's keep focused, Gallagher. This is our last chance to scope out the Fine Arts Palace and finalize the plan for lifting the necklace."

"I'm not worried," Brett said confidently. "All of these locks in this place are simple to pick. We won't have any trouble accessing this place tonight." Along with his brooding strength, Brett was a skilled locksmith with an extensive knowledge of picking tools. From skeleton warded locks through complex modern locks, Brett was skilled at picking them all. For the nineteenth-century locks, picking was simple and would take only a few seconds to unlock.

"It's not your lock-picking skills I'm worried about. The difficulty is going to be the police …"

"Remember, constables or watchmen," Gallagher corrected, showcasing his reference knowledge of the 1890s. Gallagher, more so than other travelers, enjoyed learning and researching the details of history.

Paulson continued, "The difficulty is going to be ... the constables. They're walking around here openly and regularly. One whack of their nightsticks on our heads will not only give us some pain but likely cause tampering with this time and may cause us to de-exist."

De-existence was the fatal consequence for time travelers who interfered or attempted to alter the past. A throbbing, almost crippling pain shot through their heads as a caveat of impending and irreparable interference. Yet the past would continue as it always had, and the traveler would vanish from existence.

After a pause, Brett nodded. "Let's go inside."

As they walked to the top of the stairs, they saw a group of visitors exiting the building. The three paused on the steps to let the group pass. Two constables were trailing behind that group. The constables noticed the three travelers had stopped on the steps and were looking at the entranceway. Brett, uncontrollably, looked into the eyes of one of the constables.

"Good afternoon, gentlemen," one constable greeted, looking down from the upper step.

Brett smiled and replied, "Good afternoon."

"Are you enjoying the fair?" the constable stopped and asked.

Paulson leaned forward and replied with his scripted dialogue, designed to redirect conversations. "Yes, we're having a wonderful day. We just walked from the Midway Plaisance, where our wives and children are. We only have a short while to visit the Fine Arts Palace. Do you have the current time?"

The constable pulled out his watch and looked at the time. "Yes, it's two forty-five."

"Thank you." Paulson began moving up the steps, passing the constables. Gallagher and Brett followed, nodding and smiling at them.

The two constables watched the travelers pass and enter through the large doors before continuing down the steps. Passing two women at the bottom of the steps, both constables greeted them. "Good afternoon, ladies. Are you enjoying the fair?"

Entering the Fine Arts Palace, the three moved out of earshot of the constables. The size and exquisiteness of the central hall was astounding. Decorative Roman columns showcasing multiple world exhibits lined the long hall. Paulson motioned to move past the large model of the newly designed German Reichstag, which rested in the middle of the rotunda. Walking past the model of the domed building being constructed in Berlin, Gallagher mused at the history the Reichstag would go through over the next one hundred years. Once past the model, Paulson moved to a quiet wall at the base of the center rotunda. The echoes of voices within the dome hid their conversation.

"The place is busier than it was this morning." Paulson was becoming increasingly concerned by the number of people visiting the arts exhibition. He looked over to the rear exit. "Before we go to the Japanese Room, let's review the exit plan. Once we get the necklace tonight, we need to hightail it to that door." Paulson led with his eyes to a door off the rotunda. "The door leads to an interior passageway and then to an exterior exit about twenty yards down. Once outside, we move as fast as possible to hightail it to the train station. There's a 1:05 a.m. train leaving for Duluth, and we need to be on that train."

"If we miss the train, when's the next one?" Brett asked.

"Two days."

"We'll make the train," Brett added.

Paulson was looking around as four visitors to the fair walked by. After the group passed, he turned to the others. "The faster we get to Duluth, the faster we get to the time-portation return spot. Does everyone have their return pad?" Paulson reached into his pocket and pulled out a small metallic case the size of a deck of cards. Each traveler was provided an identical return pad that reopened the time cube, enabling the time travel. If lost or separated, any traveler could use their assigned pad to reactivate the portation time cube and return to the present time.

Brett pulled out an identical case from his pocket. "I have mine."

Gallagher was tapping his pockets, looking for his case. Finally, reaching into his back pocket, he pulled out the small metallic case. "We're all set."

"All right, let's head over to the Japanese ..." Paulson stopped midsentence, his eyes wide open.

"What? What is it?"

"That little boy over there ... he caught my eye." Paulson pointed his finger without raising his arm toward a man who was grabbing the wrist of a little boy no older than five years of age. The man was pulling the little boy so hard that the child was nearly lifted off his feet. Oblivious to the many visitors to the palace, the man was dragging the child toward the three travelers.

The man's strong Italian accent echoed within the domed rotunda. Gallagher, who was fluent in Italian, as well as German and Spanish, heard the man speaking with a combination of English and Italian. "*Stupido piccolo bastardo*, why would you do that!" The man was angry and physically pushed the child against the wall a few feet from the three travelers. The force of the push knocked the air out of the child's lungs as he hit the wall. Raising his open hand, the man swung and forcibly struck the child against the side of the head.

A sinking feeling overcame Paulson as he stared at the boy with disbelief and a rising anger, which flushed his face red.

The man grabbed the boy's hair and shook his head. "*Buono a niente.* Wait until you get home. You will get it!"

Paulson began to move toward the Italian man.

Suddenly, Gallagher was overcome by a crippling migraine headache. Instinctively, he held up hands to his temple. Momentarily unaware of what had caused the sudden pain, he realized Paulson was going to interfere with time. "Paulson, wait," he murmured. Looking to Brett for help, he saw Brett was also holding his temple. "Brett!"

Brett heard Gallagher call to him as he instinctively grasped toward Paulson, but his reach was short. He was crippled from the searing pain shooting through his temple. "No, Robert, you can't ..."

Paulson did not hear Brett or Gallagher. The pain shooting through his head appeared to further enrage Paulson as he grit his teeth and moved forward. Paulson watched the tears swell in the little boy's eyes. The boy remained quiet as he fought from crying and letting his tears roll down his cheeks. Paulson's reddened face was a mixture of anger, pain, and compassion. The Italian man put his hands on his hips and then pointed to the little boy. Scolding the child in Italian, the father was again raising his hand, ready to strike.

Paulson was nearing the father and began reaching out to grab the Italian man's arm before it struck the child.

Gallagher shouted in vain. "No!"

Driven by a blind fury, Paulson was inches from grabbing the arm, but he never reached the Italian. Neither the man nor the child noticed Paulson as he attempted to stop the swing.

In a fleeting moment, Paulson vanished just as the father delivered a blow to the small child. Brett and Gallagher were in disbelief as they watched Paulson de-exist before them. There was no plume of smoke or pile of dust on the ground. In the blink of an eye, Paulson disappeared like a light being turned off.

Paulson's de-existence took Gallagher and Brett a moment to process. The two stared in shock at the place where Paulson had just stood, an empty space on the floor of the Fine Arts Palace. Still unaware of anyone else, the Italian man forcibly dragged his child away and headed toward the exit.

A small group of visitors were looking over at the commotion. Gallagher and Brett were standing frozen as someone called out, "What the devil is going on over there?"

Moving through the small group, the two constables who had greeted the travelers at the entrance had returned into the Fine Arts Palace. "What's all this?"

A woman was heard telling the constables about a man shouting at a child.

One of the constables noticed Gallagher and Brett standing motionless. The officer moved toward the two travelers. "You two, what did you see?"

Gallagher and Brett looked at each other, both without words. Gallagher was nodding and shaking his head simultaneously. The painful headache dissipated. Fighting the urge to bring attention to himself, he finally spoke. "Nothing. We didn't see anything."

The constable stared at the two questioningly. "Sit tight, you two. I'll be right back." The officer turned and walked to his partner.

Gallagher reached out to Brett and grabbed his arm. "We need to leave. The mission is over."

Brett held his hands to his forehead, still shaking off the migraine. "But we should ... I mean, could we ... I, I ..." His mind raced to what he already knew. Paulson had de-existed. He would not be coming back, nor was he returning to his home in the future. His life ended at the Fine Arts Palace in Chicago 1893. Further, the incident in the rotunda had brought a police presence, and Gallagher and Brett were no longer anonymous.

"We can't stay. We need to go now."

Brett rubbed his eyes. He saw the two constables talking and motioning toward him. He finally answered. "Yes ... we need to go."

The two understood and followed the protocol for a failed mission. Quietly exit and return back to the PTE Unit Complex in the present day. The missing jade necklace would forever remain lost in time.

Chapter 2
The PTE Unit Complex

There is a moment during time-portation that provides the traveler with an accelerated feeling in the stomach, almost like a roller coaster ride going down that first slope. However, when Brett and Gallagher returned from 1893 to the present day, the portation did not leave a sensation in the stomach. Both Miles Gallagher and Michael Brett remained stunned and saddened by the de-existence of their friend, Robert Paulson.

The two departed Chicago aboard the train to the portation return spot, north of Duluth, Minnesota. After opening the time cube, the two portated to the present day and boarded a flight to Seattle to return to their Past Time Evacuators Unit. Without the jade necklace or their colleague, the two quietly returned to the PTE Unit Complex outside Seattle. Any mission ran the risk of interference with time, and de-existing was a known hazard. Nevertheless, the moment could not be prepared for and remained etched on the memory of the two men.

Arriving in Seattle, Gallagher and Brett were met at the airport by a PTE military escort. As was the custom upon returning from a mission, the military escort wore camouflage clothing with only two stripes on the sleeve indicating the rank of corporal. The greeting was formal, and no names were exchanged. Entering the unmarked black sedan, they drove an hour northward to the PTE Unit Complex.

The PTEUC was constructed in the northern part of Washington State at latitude 47° north, also known as the forty-seventh parallel. The latitudinal line crosses three continents, allowing the travelers to move between North America, Europe, and Asia along the latitude line.

The time device transported travelers within the troposphere as Earth spun along the forty-seventh parallel. The unit's main computer, housed in the time console, adjusted to the changes in geographic height and the planet's orbit around the sun, ensuring the travelers were never transported into harm's way. Travelers never feared arriving in the middle of outer space when the planet was on the other side of the sun or inside of a mountain when moving from sea level to higher ground.

The Past Time Evacuators Unit was a military-controlled operation, housed within a modified military distribution center. The PTEUC was divided into three units of operation: the travelers, the researchers, and the military. Gallagher and Brett were assigned as travelers. To minimize relationships from developing from other units of the PTE operation, the travelers were kept secluded from most of the researchers and military. On those occasions when interaction occurred, Gallagher or Brett rarely knew the names of those they were interacting with, including their military escort from the airport.

The driver arrived at the PTEUC, entering a long, enclosed tunnel that separated the different units of operation. They passed the military unit, which housed the internal barracks, mess hall, and armory. Further down the tunnel was the research unit, including a warehouse of time period items, clothing, and supplies. At the end of the tunnel was the travelers unit.

The travelers unit was made of three unique PTE sectors. Sector one was the portation room, which housed the time-travel console that would send travelers along the forty-seventh parallel. Sector two was the library room, where no books were stored but was used as the central research and distribution center. The library held three long lab tables, a large map table, and several interactive computer monitors to allow the travelers to prepare for missions. Sector three was the travelers' quarters, which included the colonel's office, the travelers' private quarters, and a reception lounge area with an adjoining kitchen and washrooms.

The corporal parked the black sedan in the tunnel outside the travelers unit. The colonel's adjunct, whom Gallagher and Brett only knew as "Sergeant Major," met the two at the door. His uniform, like the corporal's, did not have a name stenciled on the operational camouflage breast pocket. Only the sergeant major insignia, with a star surrounded by stripes designating the rank, was sewn into his upper sleeves. "Thank you, Corporal," the sergeant major told the escort. "You're excused."

As their military escort left, the sergeant major stretched his arm out and pointed to the colonel's office. "The colonel is expecting you."

The PTE commander was Colonel Tatiana Mangrove, who oversaw the entire PTE operation. Although the travelers did not hold a commissioned military post, they were classified as "government experimental personnel" and supervised, managed, and directed by Colonel Mangrove. Her slender frame did not reflect her strength in leading. She was a decisive leader, confident in her abilities as the head of the operation for the past two years.

Upon entering the colonel's office, Brett and Gallagher were motioned to sit by the colonel, who remained seated. She maintained a high standard of dress and appearance, her military uniform spotless and her hair secured in a ponytail. Once seated, Gallagher and Brett provided her with a summary of the World's Fair mission. The colonel listened to the report of Paulson's heroic yet detrimental actions. "Then the police arrived. We were about to be interrogated. That's when we abandoned the mission."

After finishing the report, Gallagher and Brett looked exhausted and drained.

The colonel sat upright in her chair as she considered her words. She had stroked a strand of her auburn hair over her ear. "I understand what Mr. Paulson did."

Gallagher and Brett both looked up in surprise. The colonel rarely engaged in personal conversations, preferring to remain focused on PTE missions.

The colonel leaned forward on her chair. "Mr. Paulson grew up in an abusive environment," she explained bluntly. "He might have, at that moment, acted upon pure instinct."

Brett shook his head. "We just watched. I did nothing. Maybe we should have—"

The colonel cut Brett off. "Mr. Brett, you did nothing because there was nothing you could have done. Abandoning the mission was the right decision."

Before Brett could reply, the colonel rose and walked from behind the desk. "You both know that it is critical to stay within the mission parameters and avoid interference when possible. The further you stray, the greater the risk of de-existing." She leaned against her desk. "Mr. Paulson, above anyone else, knew the risks. He knew our focus ... our goals. And he was keenly aware of the perils of interfering with history on any mission. As are you."

Gallagher echoed her words. "Yeah, perils."

"We will need to do some notifications and make arrangements. In the meantime, I'd like you two to go to your quarters and get some rest." The colonel tapped her index finger three times on the desk. "If, after resting, you're ready to return, I would like to brief you on the mission. We have updated information on a new artifact."

"Another mission?" Gallagher asked.

The colonel moved to her office door. "Yes, another mission that I'd like to begin as soon as possible. I'm meeting with Dr. Foster later. I'll also update him on the Chicago details. After you rest, I'll have Dr. Foster check on your readiness. If you need more time, I'll see to it that it's allowed. If, however, you are ready to begin another mission, Dr. Foster will arrange for a briefing to bring you up to speed."

The colonel opened her office door and called to her adjunct. "Sergeant Major, will you escort Mr. Gallagher and Mr. Brett to their quarters?"

"Yes, ma'am." The colonel's adjunct promptly entered the office. "Gentlemen, this way, please." The sergeant major pointed to the lounge area outside the office.

Gallagher and Brett stood and followed the sergeant major toward their private quarters adjacent to the reception lounge in the travelers' unit of the PTEUC. Passing through the lounge, Gallagher and Brett noticed that a meal was set for them at the kitchen table. The sergeant major walked to the table and pulled out two chairs for them. Realizing their hunger, the two sat down and quietly ate. As their stomachs filled, Gallagher and Brett soon grew tired.

Chapter 3
The New Mission

The colonel had been correct about the need for rest. Following the meal, Gallagher and Brett entered their respective quarters and slept deeply. The following day, Gallagher felt rested and had his energy back. As he sat up in bed, he thought about the idea of a new mission. For each mission, there was the excitement of a challenging goal to retrieve lost artifacts from the past. Although his emotions were mixed with the sadness of losing a colleague, Gallagher was an adventurer by nature and lived for different quests. At a young age, he left home to travel mainland Europe, seeking the excitement that crossed his path. Upon recruitment to the PTE and undertaking his role as a traveler, Gallagher had finally felt a sense of purpose. Feeling reinvigorated, he walked out to the reception lounge.

Brett was standing in the kitchen, pouring a cup of coffee. He turned to see Gallagher walk out of his room. "Foster was just here," he said.

Scanning the reception lounge for Foster, Gallagher replied, "Where did he go?"

"I told him I felt good and was up for hearing the colonel's briefing of the new mission if you were. He said he'd speak with her and come back to check on you."

During their time together, Gallagher and Brett had successfully completed twelve time-travel trips, working with either Robert Paulson or Dr. Nikodem Foster. Foster did not like the name "Nick" or the use of his academic title, as his doctorate was in engineering, not medical. He maintained his modesty by asking that he be referred to the same way as all the travelers by their last name, rarely using first names. Although

Foster had knowledge of thermomagnetic time travel and had worked with the inventor of the time-travel console, Dr. Angler, he favored being a traveler.

Foster was smiling as he entered the lounge. "Gallagher! I'm glad to see you're up."

Gallagher gave a chuckle, as he knew Foster was giving him a jab about sleeping more than the others. "Bright-eyed and bushy-tailed," he retorted.

"Look, I'm terribly saddened to hear about Paulson. The colonel updated me and has directed arrangements to be made at the end of the month." Foster moved over to a lounge chair and sat down. "I knew Paulson for a long time, and I wish I could have been there."

"I'm not sure there was anything you could have done … or that we could have done," Gallagher replied.

"Probably not," Foster sighed. "I had known about his past trauma and abuse. He didn't like to talk about his past, but it was always there. I know he couldn't have allowed a child to be hit in front of him."

"We didn't know," Gallagher added. "It happened so fast."

Foster nodded. "If done all over again, I'm not sure he would've done anything different." Foster stood back up. "We all have things that make up our character that we can't define. Call them primal instincts or core values. But it is those things that make up our individuality. Paulson … was doing what he needed to do."

"Maybe." Gallagher had a tone of anger to his sadness.

"Michael, in all likelihood, by doing anything to stop Paulson, you would have also been interfering. You would have only brought more attention to yourself, possibly having the police detain the two of you. Those actions might have caused all three of you to de-exist. We all know how risky the stakes are on a mission. Robert Paulson above anybody else." Foster echoed the travelers' calling.

Brett and Gallagher looked at each for a moment.

Foster leaned his hands onto the kitchen table. "We all know the risks. We also know our job as travelers and our role in the PTE."

The three quietly reflected on their calling as time travelers. Brett finally broke the silence. "So ... we were told there's a new mission."

Foster looked at the two and gave a small smile. "Yes. One that is immediate if you're ready."

Brett stood. "I'm ready."

Gallagher stood too. "I'm good. What's the new mission?"

"The colonel wants to lead the briefing. She and Maurice are in the library waiting. They have something more challenging than we had previously experienced."

"Will Maurice have his research team too?"

"Just Maurice." Foster gave a serious look. "But his research team has come up with something big. Something our skills are needed for."

"As opposed to what we did before?" Brett chirped.

"It's the artifact that's big."

"What is it?"

"It's best if the colonel and Maurice explain our mission." Foster causally pointed to the door.

Gallagher jumped in. "Come on, Foster, what is it?"

Foster stood straight up. "It's best to hear it from the colonel and Maurice. Let's get to the library and find out."

Chapter 4
Map One of Two

Once at the library, the colonel greeted Foster, Gallagher, and Brett. She was standing next to a large touchscreen monitor, alongside the head of the research unit, Maurice. Behind the colonel were various items spread onto a library table. Maurice stood up from the computer as the three travelers entered, glaring at them over his half-rim glasses. Maurice, along with the PTE research team, provided the colonel with the recommended missions from their research of artifacts that were missing or lost in time.

"Good morning, gentlemen," the colonel began, refocused on a new mission. "Please move to the computer. Mr. Maurice will provide you with background information on the next mission."

Maurice sat down and clicked the computer screen, showing various information windows. "The artifact we will attempt to recover is a lost treasure from World War II." He smiled with pride as he tapped the screen to enlarge an image. "We have been searching for over a year for this spectacular lost treasure. This is a photograph of the Eighth Wonder of the Modern World."

The image showed a vintage photograph that appeared to have been originally black and white and then hand-painted. The caption underneath stated, "The Amber Room of Catherine Palace." Maurice looked at the colonel, awaiting her directive to continue.

The colonel, who now stood to the side of the monitor, raised her arm for Maurice to continue. Maurice strolled to the monitor and pointed to the photograph. "It was known famously as the Amber Room. The walls were gilded and carved with thousand-pound amber panels. Those panels were decorated with gold and adorned with gemstones."

The colonel interjected, "The Amber Room was last displayed in the Catherine Palace outside of St. Petersburg, Russia, in 1944."

Maurice continued, "The room was originally constructed in Berlin. But after a visit from Peter the Great, he desired the room to be relocated to Russia in 1716, where it remained until World War II." Maurice tapped on the screen to bring up an overview of Catherine Palace. "At the end of the German occupation, the Amber Room was dismantled and stolen by the Nazis." Swiping the computer screen, another image appeared to show a photograph of a Nazi officer. "This is a photograph of Erich Koch, who was the *Gauleiter*, or regional leader, of East Prussia between 1928 and 1944. Koch was the officer who ordered the Amber Room to be dismantled."

"Was it taken back to Berlin after dismantling?" Gallagher asked.

"Mr. Gallagher," the colonel interjected, "let Mr. Maurice finish, and then you may ask questions."

Maurice did not wait for Gallagher to respond. "We believe Koch hid the Amber Room at a secret location somewhere in East Prussia. In 1944, at the end of World War II, Hitler directed Koch to disassemble the room. Yet the room was not sent to Berlin, and there is no transport record of where it was sent. Koch was imprisoned and interrogated for years regarding the Amber Room. But he never revealed the location. History recorded the Amber Room as a lost treasure."

"Until now," the colonel added. "We have discovered a lead on the location of the amber panels."

Maurice swiped the screen to bring up another black-and-white photograph. "This is Wolfgang Müller of Stuttgart, Germany. Müller worked under Koch in the late 1920s and into the early 1930s. While Koch was governing Nazi operations in East Prussia, he was also looting art, gold, and whatever treasures he could get his hands on, and Müller was aware of the pillaging."

"The Nazis were certainly known to pillage," Brett said under his breath.

Ignoring the comment, Maurice continued. "As Koch pillaged, Müller kept inventory records of the stolen treasures while he worked in East Prussia." Maurice clicked the screen, and a German inventory list appeared. "We uncovered a portion of Müller's record logs from 1933." Maurice zoomed in on the German document. "The handwriting on the log is attributed to Müller. The log recorded items that Koch pillaged and stole, including artwork and jewelry."

The colonel pointed to the log of items. "Müller listed the item and quantity in the first two columns. In the next column, he included the routing information. Either *nach Berlin* or *lagerraumkarte*."

Gallagher translated. "*Nach Berlin* means 'to Berlin.' The first part of the next word, *lagerraum*, means 'storage room.'"

"It could also mean 'storehouse.' Müller's note denotes whether the stolen items are shipped to Berlin or to a storehouse, or storage room. Do you know the other word?" the colonel asked.

Gallagher nodded. "*Karte* means 'map.' The two words together translate to 'storage room map.' Or 'storehouse map' if you prefer."

Maurice was nodding. "Yes, 'map.' Müller refers to a map where the items were sent."

"What are the items that Koch sent to his storehouse map?" Foster asked.

"There were two items on this log that Müller noted *lagerraumkarte*. A gold-mounted nephrite vase and an Ilya Repin painting titled *Ivan Outside*."

Foster was familiar with the painter Repin. "Koch was bold to hide the more expensive items from his bosses."

"Brave or greedy," Gallagher added.

"There is another connection to Müller." The colonel stepped back from the screen. "Not only did he work as Koch's bookkeeper, but he also served as a cartographer. Müller kept a log as well as created maps to the storage locations in East Prussia."

Maurice tapped on Müller's photograph. "Müller maintained the inventory and the map location of Koch's pillaging during the early 1930s. However, the ways things changed quickly before the war, Müller and Koch went separate ways. Koch had a rapid rise of promotions and soon had a much more important role in the Nazi party, while Müller was left out. Müller returned to Berlin in 1935, where he worked as a cartographer at the Berlin Institute of Technology."

Gallagher translated the university to German. "*Die Technische Universität Berlin.*"

The colonel glanced toward Gallagher. "Yes."

Maurice continued, "In the university archive, we discovered a series of Müller's detailed and handcrafted maps. The maps were general in context, such as mainland European countries or towns, with the exception of one map." Maurice stood and moved past the colonel over to the library table. He carefully picked a rolled-up sheet and unrolled the aged paper to reveal a hand-drawn map. "This map differed from the other maps."

Maurice delicately turned the unrolled map to allow Foster, Gallagher, and Brett to see. The paper had yellowed with age, and the corners were turning brown. The map was of a remote area in East

Prussia, now part of Russia. "Looking at the date, Müller drew the map in July 1932."

"Impressive detail," Gallagher said, looking closely. "May I hold it?"

Maurice handed Gallagher the map. "Please be gentle."

Gallagher took the map and fully spread the sheet onto the library table. He held the upper corners as he studied the detail. Gallagher leaned close to the map, squinting at geographic symbols. "Müller hid a cross symbol for directions. You see here, this line has a dot, indicating north. Interesting how he wrote the legend on the side. Very deceptive."

"Yes. Müller intentionally turned the legend to misdirect," the colonel added.

"He had excellent detail. You can see on these lines he used a ruler. Yet these lines are freehand. You can pick up the subtle differences of his hand motion. Müller definitely had steady hands. There is interesting writing in the corner."

Nur E. Koch. Sonst niemand. Lagerraum - ZWEI VON ZWEI

Gallagher looked up to see Foster and Brett, who didn't understand the German words. "It means the map leads to a storage room and is only for E. Koch. And *zwei* just means the number two."

"E. Koch is *Gauleiter* Erich Koch," the colonel added. "What do you think the number two means?

Foster answered. "*Zwei von zwei* ... 'two of two.' I would think it means 'Map Two of Two.'"

"There is also writing on the back side of the map. Turn it over."

Gallagher flipped the map around.

Der Universität verboten

"'Forbidden at the university,'" Gallagher translated. He turned the map back to the top side, studied the writing, and returned to the back.

"The pen used to write *Der Universität verboten* differs from the one used on the front."

"Müller might have written the note as a reminder to not bring the map to the university," the colonel responded.

"How did the map end up there?" Brett asked.

Maurice answered, "We think Müller was attempting to make copies of the map at the university. Notice along the sides of the map that the paper has been compressed. The sheet was placed inside a press to make a copy. Müller had copy-pressing materials available at the university."

"There is no ink residue on the map." Gallagher pointed to the edges. "It looks like he was trying to make a copy without leaving any marks on the original."

"He could have hand-copied the map," Brett suggested.

"Hand-drawing is tedious. Or his hands were no longer as steady," Maurice replied. "There are finite specifics, such as the tree count between this stream and this mountainside. The map specifies the number and type of trees. To avoid errors, a copy would capture all the details."

"Or Müller was going to make multiple copies," Gallagher proposed.

"Regardless of how the map ended up at the university, have you charted where it leads?" Foster asked.

"We have. It led to a cave." The colonel was now standing next to Gallagher. "The cave was in a remote part of eastern Russia, alongside the mountain, as marked on the map."

"What was inside the cave? Any stolen treasures?" Brett asked.

"No, there was no treasure. But we did find wooden supports installed around the cave." The colonel moved over to the table and slid photographs from an envelope showing the empty cave. "The cave is cold and damp and a poor location for storage. But the wooden supports indicate the cave was being converted for storage."

Maurice moved over to the table and pointed to the cave photos. "Koch did not complete converting the cave by the end of the war. Deductively, he stored the stolen items at another location. That location must be on map one of two. Since Müller had map two of two, we could also assume he had map one as well."

"There's a gap in time between Müller leaving East Prussia and the end of the war," Brett said. "Koch pillaged the Amber Room years after Müller had moved to Berlin."

"True. Koch disassembled the Amber Room in 1944," Maurice responded. "Berlin ordered the room to be disassembled before being taken over by the Russians. However, Koch chooses to send the Amber Room to another location instead of Berlin. With limited egress from St. Petersburg, East Prussia was available. Koch must have sent the Amber Room to his secret storehouse facility. The location of the storage is on map one of two, which Müller kept with him when he returned to Berlin."

"Our mission is to return to 1937 and negotiate with Müller to obtain map one of two," the colonel said.

"How will that not cause interference with history?" Gallagher asked.

"You will be returning in time to the day Müller dies," the colonel replied. "We will use that moment to obtain the map from his home. The timing of his unfortunate death will also serve as an advantage in minimizing interference."

"How does he die?" Gallagher asked.

"He died in a house fire in 1937," Maurice answered. "The fire began at Müller's house. Along with all his papers, manuscripts, maps, and books he collected, the home burned quickly."

"Your mission is to travel to 1937 Germany at the forty-seventh parallel and travel north to Berlin, at the fifty-second parallel. Therefore, you will travel to and from Munich for arrival and the return-portation. Just before the fire takes Müller's life, make a deal with him to obtain map one of two. The map that leads to the East Prussia storehouse."

"How are we to convince Müller?" Brett added.

The colonel continued. "Müller was attempting to make copies for a reason. Possibly to take the stolen items for himself. Since he does not know about the Amber Room, as that happened after he left East Prussia, he would be only aware of the artwork and jewelry that we found on the inventory log. Our plan is to offer a trade comparable or better than that artwork in exchange for the map."

Brett shook his head. "What type of trade would this guy accept? Gold? Money?"

The colonel walked over to Brett. "Books." Her response was matter-of-fact. "We know Müller was a collector of rare maps and books. Maurice's team is securing a rare book that is equal to the value of the artwork."

Foster appeared to agree.

The colonel looked at Brett and Gallagher. "Are you ready to undertake this mission?"

Brett looked at Foster and Gallagher. "I am."

"Me too," Gallagher responded.

"Colonel," Foster said, "our team is ready."

"Excellent." The colonel nodded and glanced at her watch. "Let's determine a travel plan timeline." A disadvantage being managed by the military is the preferred time for anything to be completed was between now and five minutes ago. The colonel was no exception to that rule and preferred missions to move swiftly with competence. Once the timeline began, each unit would need to prepare their respective travel plans.

Maurice was the first to speak. "Research is confident in the information provided. We would need twenty-four hours to complete the supplies."

Foster did not look at Maurice. "Colonel," he began deliberately, "our team would like a week to collect background information and review the research done."

"A week is too long," the colonel responded.

"Why?" Brett asked.

The colonel turned to Brett but did not speak. She turned back to Foster. "Dr. Foster, we have pressing issues that are outside of your need to know. But I can assure you, the loss of Mr. Paulson has caused some concern. Our Senate oversight is placing a great deal of pressure on General Command, and as such, is placing a great deal of pressure on my office."

"I see," Foster replied.

"I'm not sure you do, Dr. Foster. I can tell you the loss of Mr. Paulson had caused great concern about the operation continuing. The only reason we are not suspending activity is the Amber Room." The colonel turned to Maurice. "Mr. Maurice's belief in the map became my belief. And it was my belief and my convincing that has bought us time. But I am certain the time we have is limited."

Foster held back from showing concern. "How long do we have?"

"I will provide the general staff and Senate subcommittee an update in four days. Time travel does not help with the real-time issues we have." The colonel turned back to Brett. "And, Mr. Brett, in answer to your question, this complex comes with a cost from our government benefactors. If we are unable to provide a return on that investment, the measure of our cost-effectiveness is in question."

Brett looked down at the ground. "I understand."

"Now, Dr. Foster," the colonel continued, "tell me again your thoughts on a timeline?"

Foster looked over to Gallagher and Brett. Brett was still looking down. Gallagher nodded in support of Foster's decision. "We would like seventy-two hours but could do our review of information in forty-eight."

The colonel appeared to refrain from showing disdain. "I see," she said. "A completion of your task within forty-eight hours, executed with competence and confidence, would be the preferred outcome."

Without hesitation, Foster responded, "Understood."

She looked at her watch again. "It's now 1530. Mr. Maurice, please begin the supply and clothing lists. Once the clothing options are available, immediately forward to the travelers for fitting. Dr. Foster, I want your team to prepare by reviewing 1930s Munich and Berlin. To maximize your time, I suggest Mr. Gallagher review the Berlin map while you review Munich. We will reconvene tomorrow at 1500 hours for an update, to determine if additional time is needed."

Chapter 5
Travel Plans

The following afternoon, Foster, Gallagher, and Brett walked into the library fifteen minutes early to find the colonel and Maurice already waiting. The three travelers had received their clothes surprisingly early in the morning from the research team. As with any mission, the colonel required the travelers to first suit up in the appropriate wardrobe prior to reviewing the travel items.

The three dressed in the period clothing and found each outfit fit well. Each wore gray suits with matching vests, solid-black ties, and similar black ankle boots. The only noticeable difference was Foster's suit was striped, while the others were solid. Foster also had a brown overcoat, while Brett and Gallagher wore black overcoats.

Maurice, who managed the research team, represented the unit for the meeting and would oversee the direct assignment of equipment and clothes for the travelers. The research team ensured the materials and items provided to the travelers were time appropriate and minimized exposing modern technology to the past. The more modern the clothes or equipment, the higher the probability of de-existence. For the meeting, Maurice was wearing a pure-white lab coat over his wrinkled shirt. He was looking over various items spread out on the long library table.

The colonel stood next to Maurice. She was inspecting a large, leatherbound book that appeared well aged. Gallagher assumed the book was going to be used to trade for the map. The colonel turned to the three when they entered and slid the book into a covered leather sleeve. Once the book was stored, she immediately began looking over the wardrobe.

After a few minutes, she nodded in approval. "Well done on the clothing, Maurice."

"Thank you," Maurice simply responded.

"The suits look very fitting."

Maurice walked over to Foster. "I hope you noticed all three of the overcoats have inside pockets on both sides." As on all missions, this allowed the travelers to conceal items if necessary.

Brett leaned in between Foster and Maurice. "Yes, we did."

"Magnificent." The colonel refocused the conversation. "We want to begin by providing updates, beginning with research. Maurice, please update the team on Müller's family background."

Maurice cleared his throat. "He was unmarried and had no children. His only living family member in 1937 was his brother, who lived out west near Dusseldorf. Their relationship did not appear to be close. There was no mention of him in his obituary, nor were there any friends."

"There were no associates from the university?"

"None uncovered," Maurice said. "Müller's life was that of a recluse, a combination of cataloging cartography at the Berlin university and book collecting. Otherwise, there is no indication that he was social. We believe Müller lived a solitary life."

"What about neighbors?" Brett asked.

"Müller lived on a predominantly business street made up of offices and some storefronts. There were no neighbors, as there were no homes on his street. For the mission, you are to arrive in the evening, when the work community has closed their offices or shops for the day. There should be no one other than Müller at home. Further, there were no witnesses or evidence that anyone was with him the night of the fire."

"Anything else on what caused the fire?" Foster asked.

Maurice answered, "The news articles and obituary of the times reported the cause as unknown. The fire occurred the evening of September 30 or the morning of October 1. You will be traveling to Munich early Thursday, September 30, to allow you time to travel to Berlin."

"Did you find out if the map was in his house?" Gallagher asked.

The colonel gave a slight nod and continued, "Not definitely, but we believe he kept his hand-drawn maps at his house. From the Berlin reports of the fire, the home was filled with a multitude of paper and books. Likely, Müller kept his personal maps along with his book collection in his home office. You are to arrive a few hours before the fire, in the early evening, and make a deal to obtain the map. Mr. Gallagher, will you be able to recognize an East Prussian map drawn by Müller?"

"Yes, I believe so," Gallagher responded. "I'll know for sure when I see the map and can confirm the location depicted on the map."

"Just secure the map to the best of your ability, and let me worry about confirming the location." The colonel paused to gather her thoughts. "For this mission, be frank with Müller. Let him know that we are aware of Koch's pillaging and theft. Sharing your insight may accelerate his willingness to make the trade. Convince him that we need the map to regain what has been stolen."

"Too bad about the limited amount of time." Foster sighed. "Would it be better to go earlier, before the fire?"

"To minimize interference, it's best to interact with him at the end of his life. The timing of his death allows our ability to be frank—there won't be enough time for him to report our conversation to others."

"Sounds like we're literally playing with fire," Brett added.

The colonel ignored the comment. "Let's move over to the table and go over your transport items." Foster, Gallagher, and Brett stepped closer to the long center table. The colonel walked to the other side and stood near the large leatherbound book. "All right, Mr. Maurice, please provide an update on the travel supplies."

Maurice went to the large book with a deliberate, slow walk. He had an arrogance about him that irritated Gallagher. After all the times the two had met, Gallagher never knew if Maurice was his first name or last. He assumed Maurice was too smug to ever share his personal details. "Let's begin with the most important item." Maurice delicately picked up the covered leather sleeve and held the book vertically on the table. "We did a 3-D printing of an extremely rare Gutenberg Bible. The replica copy is volume one of the two-volume Bible set. The partial Gutenberg Bible was generated from an original printing from 1455. The value of the original book, even as a partial collection, is more valuable than the Repin painting listed on the log. You will use the Bible to trade for the map."

"A replica?"

"A perfect copy," Maurice said proudly. Maurice slid the Bible from its covered leather sleeve. The large book was nearly a foot and half tall. The Bible was covered with brown calfskin, and its replicated age was apparent with the delicacy of the book. "The Gutenberg is well known as the first European printed book. Gutenberg printed two volumes of the Holy Bible. Volume one will be very tantalizing for any German citizen, let alone a book collector."

"But it's a copy," Brett added.

Maurice shook his head. "It won't be an issue. No one will be able to tell it's a fake. The 3-D printing has raised ink, and the replica vellum would not be detectable in 1937."

Foster understood what the book was for. "Do you think Müller will trade the Bible for the—"

The colonel snapped a response before he finished his sentence. "Yes. Being a German, Müller will be keenly aware of the value of the Gutenberg Bible. He will see this volume as extremely valuable and of greater worth than the items in storage. Also, Müller is an aficionado of rare books."

Foster continued, "I only ask because if we bring something additional, we could sweeten the pot if he is apprehensive. Should we print volume two and bring both?"

"I don't think so," Maurice responded. "There are only about fifty Gutenberg Bibles that existed in 1937, many being partial. Therefore, having a partial collection would be more convincing."

"What is the value of the volume in the 1930s?" Brett asked.

Maurice stared at the book. "Volume one would probably be valued at $15,000, give or take."

"So, about a quarter of a million in today's dollars," Gallagher added. His ability to do mental inflation calculations always impressed Foster.

Foster was hesitant. "That's expensive, but I wonder if it's a large enough carrot?"

The colonel became insistent. "Precisely the reason why you arrive in the early evening: to give you as much time as possible. We will implement an alternate plan if needed. In the event you are unsuccessful, withdraw from the mission and return to our time. We will review what you learned during the interaction and adjust as necessary. If he is apprehensive, do not hold back learning what price he will take to trade the map. Then you have the last few hours of the night before the fire begins, to make another attempt."

"Should we discuss that plan now?"

"Unnecessary. If needed, which I don't believe it will be, we will review Müller's reaction and conversation in the event you withdraw. But the man is a known collector of rare books. The Gutenberg will work."

"Okay." Foster looked at Brett and Gallagher. Both shrugged their shoulders with biddable approval. "Maurice, what else do you have for us?"

Maurice returned the Gutenberg Bible back into the leather sleeve. He then placed the sleeve into a black leather briefcase. "The book should stay in the sleeve until you're ready to trade. It will be carried in the briefcase. If asked to open the case, there's a stack of lumber transport logs along with a few days of the *Münchener Post* newspaper from that time."

"Is the briefcase disposable, or does it need to return?" Foster asked.

"The lumber logs are meaningless, and the briefcase is time appropriate. You do not need to return the case, as it will not pose a threat if left behind. As long as you remove the Gutenberg."

"I'll remember," Foster said with seriousness.

Maurice looked back at the items on the table. "Here are your travel orders and *Pässe* or German passports with your aliases. You will need to carry them in your suit pocket. Please review those details in the event that you are stopped; 1937 is prewar, so it may not be as intense as the years to follow. Nevertheless, keep the papers on you at all times. Additionally, there are Reichsmarks for you to purchase train tickets and meals."

"To enjoy authentic German apple strudel," Gallagher added.

Maurice paused and stared at Gallagher for a moment. The eyes did not show any emotion, but Gallagher thought Maurice was filled with disdain. The colonel noticed the stare-down and continued to avoid any awkwardness. "For this trip, Dr. Foster is the lead, but all interactions with citizens are to be done by Mr. Gallagher because of his fluent German."

"*Das stimmt. Ich spreche wunderbar Deutsch.*"

The colonel nodded, clearly not knowing what Gallagher said. "Mr. Brett, your role is to actively monitor for any interference and, if needed, access locked areas. On the table, you will find the 1930s pocket toolkit and lockpicks. The toolkit is more modern than the picks you used in Chicago."

"No problem," Brett said confidently.

"Be cognizant of the many variables in Nazi Germany, including unfriendlies, such as the Gestapo. Müller lives on the outside of Berlin, so it will not be as heavily traveled as it is near the Reich Chancellery. But keep your guard up. You need to constantly remember where you are. Keep the team focused on the mission and blend in."

Brett nodded. "I understand."

The colonel looked at Foster. "Mr. Gallagher," she continued, "be fluid and adjust as necessary when speaking with Müller. Dr. Foster, when you arrive along the forty-seventh parallel, you will be just outside Munich. From there, take the train to Berlin. Once in Berlin, take the Berliner streetcar as far northeast as possible. You will have to walk another mile to Mauser Strah-be, where Müller's house is located."

"It's pronounced *Mauserstrasse*," Gallagher corrected.

"Mauser Street is where Müller lives. It's on the outer part of the city." The colonel looked at Gallagher. "Remember, have Mr. Gallagher do the talking, purchasing tickets, and ordering meals. Do you have questions?"

"I'm good." Foster turned to Gallagher and Brett. "Any questions?"

Both shook their heads.

The colonel nodded. "Are you able to complete your review of Munich and Berlin in the next twenty-four hours?"

Foster did not wait for a response from either Gallagher or Brett. "Yes, we're on schedule. We will be ready to depart in twenty-four hours."

The colonel nodded. "Very well," she began. "We will schedule the portation to take place at 1600 hours departure. Between now and then, please review the pertinent information for Munich, Berlin, and Müller." The colonel scanned the room. No one spoke. "If there is nothing else, I will meet you tomorrow at the portation room."

As the colonel walked from the room with Maurice following, Gallagher turned to Foster and Brett. *"Wir reisen nach München."*

Foster partially understood the German language. "Yes, we're off to Munich, 1937 Nazi Germany Munich specifically."

Chapter 6
Portation Room

The colonel led the way into the portation room. Foster carried the briefcase holding the Gutenberg Bible to his side while Maurice quietly followed from behind. Gallagher and Brett entered the room last. The portation room was a larger room devoid of color other than a sterile off-white paint. The focus of the room was the PTE console, more commonly known as the time generator, positioned slightly off center in the room. The generator had a multiphase control console, which housed a keyboard and a small monitor, and four laser emitters within tubular frames, which pointed to the exterior portation pad rods.

    At the top of the tubes, reflectors were braced to the four tubes in a perpendicular fashion. Each reflector pointed to a second set of rods which, when turned on, generated the time cube portation. The time cube encapsulated travelers by creating an enclosed and controlled transport, which would ping-pong along the timestream. The portation opened the timestream for travelers to go present-to-past and past-to-present. As the future had not yet become history, time travelers only visited the past.

    Against the wall of the portation room was a black-countered clean-up sink with a series of four chairs. Gallagher sat down to tighten his boot laces. As he tightened his laces, Maurice passed him and walked along a large insulated electric cable that ran from the time generator to a steel switch box that powered the unit. He pulled the switch up, and the generator hummed as electricity filled the device. Turning toward the travelers, Maurice pulled out three small metal cases from his lab coat. The cases were similar to the pads Brett and Gallagher had used to return from 1893.

"Here are your return pads," Maurice said. "You will arrive in rural Germany, six klicks outside Munich's city center," Maurice said, looking over the top of his half-rim glasses. "Any of the three pads may be used to reopen the time cube." He handed Gallagher and Brett each a return pad. Maurice then opened the third case and showed the three the internal controls. "The LCD clock will adjust to the time of your location. You want to adjust your wristwatches accordingly. The blue light on the right will be lit solid if the transportation is successful. If the time or location differs from what we programmed, the blue light will either blink or not turn on. If that occurs, lock your coordinates by holding the two outer buttons. Then set the return button and come back here."

We know, Gallagher thought to himself.

Maurice held the open case toward Gallagher and Brett. "Push this button down and then slide it to the right. Hold it for five seconds and release. That will activate the time generator to reopen the time cube."

Gallagher smiled as Maurice held the case at them for several seconds without talking. He, as well as Foster and Brett, knew how to operate the return pad. Gallagher thought Maurice was patronizing the three travelers.

Finally, Maurice pointed to a small dim light in the corner of the internal controls. "When this light is flashing, you're outside of the return cube. You have to position yourself so the light is solid, otherwise, the cube will not form for the return."

"May I have mine?" Foster asked.

Without responding, Maurice handed Foster the return pad to the hand holding the briefcase. Foster switched the case to his other hand. He took the return pad and placed it in his inner jacket pocket.

"Gentlemen," the colonel said with authority, "we're all set. Safe travels."

Without further discussion, Foster, Gallagher, and Brett walked onto the transportation pad. Gallagher stared at Maurice, who walked to the keyboard at the control console. The rectangular console was built within a bronze metallic body rising four feet off the ground, where the keyboard and monitor rested. The shafts of the four lasers were set on a rotating axis. The rotation of the device was set to meet the reflectors on top of the tubes. On the sides of the shaft were smaller lasers, capable only of lateral pivoting to interlock the time cube.

The colonel stood outside the transportation array while Maurice completed the inputs to the time generator. He programmed it to transport the three along the forty-seventh parallel to 7:00 a.m. on September 30, 1937, approximately six kilometers east of Munich. Within moments, the console hummed loudly as the lasers emitted a cubical form within the transportation pad. The time cube was formed around the three travelers.

The lasers on the main console focused the beams surrounding the transportation circle. The colonel watched as the time generator created a visible, hazy cube around the three travelers. As the humming grew from the console, the cube clouded. The colonel and Maurice could still see the travelers, but they began to be veiled behind a gray wall that encapsulated the cube.

Gallagher looked to Maurice and smiled as the three were entirely encapsulated within the cube and transported along the timestream into the past. All three felt a sensation of acceleration; a combination of excitement and fear filled each as they began their mission.

Inside the portation room, the echoing sound from the time generator bounced off the walls as the colonel and Maurice watched the travelers vanish into the past. Moments later, the humming within the console died down and the gray cube dissipated. The cube disappeared as the lasers shut down. The colonel and Maurice stood alone, looking at the empty transportation pad.

Chapter 7
East of Munich

Once fully encapsulated in the time cube, the three travelers could only see hazy gray walls surrounding them. Although they had the sensation of transporting to another time, they did not witness any form of travel. The gray box dissipated, and the three stood in a grassy field on a brisk morning. Gallagher felt the temperature was much cooler than the portation room, and the ground was wet, as if there had been recent rain. The sun was beginning to rise on the horizon. Although the sky was only scattered with clouds, a drop of rain fell on his nose, and he momentarily twitched from the light drizzle.

Foster opened the return pad and looked at the small readout on his stainless-steel case. "We're in the right place and time. The light is solid blue, so we're just east of Munich on September 30, 1937." Looking around the grassy field, there was not a building or person in sight. The dawn's light revealed trees in the distance. The leaves had changed to an orangish brown as summer turned into fall. The air was fresh, and the smell of diesel fuel and war machines was still a few years away. He then clasped the case and looked at his watch. "It's 7:08 a.m., Berlin time. There's an 11:00 a.m. train to Berlin that we want to catch."

"Which direction do we head?" Gallagher asked.

Foster looked at his watch again, which had a compass around the outer band of the face. "We go due west. There's a road nearby that will lead to the city."

Brett added, "Hopefully it's not too far of a walk."

"Just under four miles. Let's start walking, and we'll be able to catch the train without a problem."

Brett followed Foster across the wet grass. "We're cutting things so close. I wonder if we should have arrived two days early rather than one to meet with Müller."

"You know what the colonel said. Keep the mission within limited times and cut this visit as close as possible," Foster said, walking toward the trees in the distance. "To minimize the chance of de-existing, we keep a tight schedule."

Gallagher walked next to Brett as they crossed the field. "We know Müller dies in a fire late tonight. There's not much time, so I hope our plan to negotiate with him works."

"If not, we return to the portation room and go with plan B," Foster replied. "But let's focus on plan A. Look up ahead. There's the road just past those trees. It leads to Munich."

The three walked across the field, and the wet grass soaked through their shoes. As they approached the trees near the road, Brett heard a car in the distance. "Should we try to catch a ride?"

"No, we need to keep a low profile." Foster pointed to nearby trees. "Move behind the trees, and let's wait for the car to pass." Getting under cover, the three waited. After the car passed without noticing the three hidden figures, Foster walked back into the open. "Let's go."

The trees gave way to a ditch, which ran alongside the small road going east and west. The three stretched across the ditch to avoid stepping into the retained water. Upon reaching the road, they stopped and listened. They heard nothing. Foster looked at the compass of his watch. "This way." Foster began walking toward town, and the two followed.

Chapter 8
Munich to Berlin

The six-kilometer walk to Munich was draining on Gallagher as the drizzle continued to moisten his face throughout the journey. His ankle boots, although time-period appropriate, did not offer the comfort of modern shoes. After forty-five minutes of walking, the countryside of Germany was replaced with buildings and houses as they entered the outskirts of Munich. Once in the city center, Foster led the three to a main road, where Gallagher purchased three tickets to ride a streetcar to the train station, known as the München Hauptbahnhof.

As they rode the streetcar deeper into Munich, there were signs of the times. Although they did not see the black uniforms of the infamous Secret State Police, *Geheime Staatspolizei*, more commonly known as the Gestapo, the three observed armed guards wearing the field-green color of the Wehrmacht. Citizens moved through the city, but there was a peculiar quietness to them.

The München Hauptbahnhof was located in the heart of Munich. Upon arriving at the train station, the three travelers prepared their identification documents and paperwork to show to the authorities. The paperwork related to their apparent work in the automation of a tool-and-die-making company that was a subsidiary of Dornier Flugzeugwerke. Their cover story was working on cable fastener clips that were produced in Berlin and shipped to Munich to the main plant. The hope was the story was convincing if asked yet meaningless to prying ears. However, upon purchasing the tickets, the ticketing agent only requested their identification cards to be shown. Gallagher paid with the Reichsmarks, and the tickets were issued without question. "*Dánke.*"

The three unobtrusively boarded the train without discussion. They sat in seats facing each other, and Brett sat nearest to the window to avoid conversation if needed. Foster opened the briefcase, pulled out the newspaper, and pretended to read the German articles. The only conversation was with the conductor who checked their tickets. To minimize interaction, the three held off from eating or using the washroom en route to Berlin. They quietly sat in their seats, often looking out the window at the passing countryside.

	Along the journey, the train passed through Nuremberg. Gallagher found it difficult not to think of what was to happen in the next decade with Germany, which would conclude with a yearlong trial held in that city. After several hours, the train arrived at the Berlin Anhalter Bahnhof. Although there were visible armed guards present at the train station, the travelers were left alone as they exited the building. The sun would soon be setting as the three walked onto the street and away from the Berlin Anhalter Bahnhof. Walking to a north-south street, the travelers boarded a streetcar and rode north toward Müller's house.

	As they traveled on the streetcar, dusk began to fall. Fewer and fewer people were seen on the street. Reaching the northernmost stop of the streetcar, the three exited along with one other passenger. The passenger, an older man carrying a bag of groceries, was quick to exit and walk from the streetcar.

	The streetcar reversed direction and returned south. Glancing toward the man, Gallagher noticed him scurry down the street and hurry round the corner, leaving the three travelers alone. Standing under the dark sky, Gallagher felt a sense of foreboding, being outside in the darkness of prewar Nazi Germany.

"Even though unseen, there is no doubt German authorities are nearby," Foster whispered as he watched the streetcar disappear into the night. "Come on and stay close to the buildings and use the shadows to hide as much as possible. And be very quiet."

No kidding, Gallagher thought to himself. He felt his heart racing. Although they were not in immediate danger, Gallagher felt they were doomed if caught by the Nazis. Continuing to look down the street in both directions, he saw no sign of anyone.

Walking down to the closest street corner, Foster slowed to look around in search of street patrols. At one point, an automobile could be heard several blocks away. The three waited and listened. The noise of the car became distant, and they resumed their trek.

To play down his fears, Gallagher pointed to a street sign bolted to the side of a building: Kastanie Straße. "This part of Berlin is very symmetrical. Only three blocks."

"Good," Foster replied. "We're close."

On the way to Müller's house, sunset changed to twilight and darkness. Foster led Gallagher and Brett in a straight line, keeping close to the buildings. An uneasy feeling was shared as they continued to hear and see no one. Gallagher wondered if there was something going on that they were unaware of. The war had not yet begun, but the Nazi tyranny still held the country in a closed fist.

Foster noticed the shared tension. "It's probably quiet because of a curfew. Let's stay vigilant and keep moving." The three were walking at a fast pace toward Müller's street. Arriving, Foster pointed to a street sign on a corner building: Mauserstraße.

Continuing the stealth tactics, along with natural caution, the three circled the street where Müller lived, to ensure they were not followed.

Müller lived on a short block full of commercial buildings and a few storefronts. His house was squeezed between two office buildings. Walking closer, the three travelers ducked into a nearby storefront. Hiding in the shadows allowed a few moments for last-minute thoughts while scoping Müller's house.

The house was surprisingly elegant among the office buildings. A low metal fence with a center gate surrounded the property of the home. A walk led to a wooden front door with an ornate window decorating the upper half. There was a small yard on the side, where a little garden grew. The two-story house was surrounded by thick bushes trimmed just below the first-floor windows. Müller lived in a strange oasis within the capital city.

On the second floor, the curtains were closed tight, but on the first floor, a three-sided bay window shone light down onto the small garden below. The garden was inside the gated area but accessible from the walkway. In the middle of the garden sat a large, manicured bush.

"Down the street ... there's an alley. Let's move over there." Foster motioned to Gallagher and Brett to follow him to the small alley a few buildings from Müller's house. The alley divided two businesses and led into the shadows of a dead end. "These businesses are closed for the day, so we can get situated without being seen. What did you make of the house?"

"Looks quiet," Gallagher said. "But the lights are on downstairs, so my guess is Müller is home."

"The front door looks somewhat inviting," Brett added. "I think we could go up and knock on the door and make the offer."

"The only thing is we may be intimidating if we all go up and knock on the door." Foster turned to Brett. "You should hang back in the alley while Gallagher and I go to the house."

"There's another option. Did you see the bush in Müller's garden?" Brett nodded at Gallagher and Foster. "It's a good size for me to hide behind. If you two get in, I'll watch what's happening inside from that garden window."

"Do you think there's enough room to hide without being seen?"

"Yes, I think so. If it's too small, I'll move quickly back to the alley."

"All right. Let's not waste any more time." Foster knelt and opened the briefcase. He moved the papers to the side and took out the covered leather sleeve that held the replica of the Gutenberg Bible. He slid the Bible out of the sleeve and handed Gallagher the book. Foster then took out the letter and travel orders from the briefcase and placed them in his coat pocket.

"Once Brett hides, you move to the front door, and I'll stand back by the gate to not look threatening. When ready, knock on the door, show him the Bible, and tell him you and I have an offer to make. Don't volunteer too much information, but if he gets suspicious, let him know we are visiting in the evening to avoid outside influences. He's welcome to search us, but ideally inside the house, to get us off the street as fast as possible. Okay?"

"Okay."

"What about the briefcase?" Brett pointed to the case sitting on the ground in the alley.

From the alley, Foster peered around the corner toward Müller's property. A garden lay in an empty lot on the west side of the building. "Okay, team," Foster began, "it's time. Are you ready?"

Brett was quick to answer. "Yes."

Gallagher nodded in agreement, answering in German. "*Ja.*"

"Then let's go forward, be on our guard, and stay focused on the mission." Foster pointed for Gallagher to begin.

Chapter 9
Wolfgang Müller

Gallagher led Foster and Brett out of the alley and toward Müller's house. He strolled casually down the street with the two following a few feet behind. Arriving outside the home, Gallagher opened the sidewalk gate. Brett crouched down and moved past Gallagher and into the shadows of the large bush in the garden.

Gallagher glanced over to the window above the garden. Dark-red curtains were drawn open, and the interior house lights were seeping through the window. He turned toward Foster, who motioned for him to go forward. Gallagher walked toward the front door while Foster stayed at the fence. *Knock on the door or tap on the side glass?* Gallagher thought, considering how to best draw Müller's attention without suspicion.

He leaned from the front door to peer into the bay window. He could see shelves filled with books. Müller's library, perhaps. At first glance, it did not look like anyone was inside the house, Gallagher thought. A moment later, he spotted a shadow moving within the library.

Gallagher glanced back to Foster. "He's inside the library," he whispered.

Foster gave a thumbs-up. "Go ahead," Foster mouthed, avoiding the use of sound.

With a deep breath, Gallagher tapped on the door with three quiet but confident knocks. A moment later, the shadow he saw earlier opened the door. The man wore a vintage smoking jacket, which at this time would likely be fashionable. "*Ja, was ist los?*"

Before talking, Gallagher lifted his hands and held out Volume One of the Gutenberg Bible. Once the man saw the exquisite book, Gallagher said in German that he had a proposition to trade the Bible. "*Ich möchte den Gutenberg umtauschen.*"

Müller peered out of the door at Gallagher and then to Foster, standing at his gate. He then looked both ways down the street. "You are American?" he asked in English.

"Yes," Gallagher said hesitantly. He lifted the Bible higher. "I would like to trade my original Gutenberg."

Müller glanced at the Bible, then toward Gallagher. "I saw you and your friends walking around my home earlier. You are not so … how do you say, spy?"

"No, we are not spies," Gallagher said, intentionally avoiding correcting Müller.

"Then why does your friend hide in the shadows of my garden?"

Before Gallagher could respond, Brett stepped forward from the bush with his hands in the air. He slowly moved next to Foster. Foster took one step forward and spoke to Müller with sincerity. "Herr Müller, we are not spies. We are here to make an offer. We brought the Gutenberg in hopes of a trade."

"Offer. This does not look like an offer. Why not come to the university and speak with me at my office?"

"Herr Müller," Foster continued, "we came to you at night to have a private conversation. We do not want any influence from outsiders."

"Outsiders?" Müller asked. "Is this why he hides in the garden?"

Foster elaborated. "He was hiding to look for any unwanted intrusions, as we are visiting in the evening. We have a very profitable offer that we would like to make. A private offer. The Gutenberg Bible in my colleague's hand … we would like to give it to you."

Müller almost laughed. "Give it to me? In exchange for what?"

"The streets might be quiet now, but that could change. If we may come in, we will let you inspect the Bible and answer any question."

Müller was hesitant. "I am a loyal National Socialist and a supporter of the Fuhrer. If you came here with a weapon …"

"We have no weapons, and you are free to check." Foster held his hands in the air, which caused his jacket to open. "We mean you no harm but only to offer this valuable Gutenberg Bible."

Müller was suspicious. "I do not fear harm, for the Staatspolizei would easily find you and put you to death if harm was to come to me."

"No, we are not here to cause harm but rather make a plea," Foster quickly replied. "We have come to speak with you privately to offer you this partial Gutenberg Bible."

Müller studied Foster. Gallagher and Brett both opened their jackets to reveal the inside. Pausing for a moment, Müller finally waved his hand for them to enter. Gallagher went inside first, followed by Foster then Brett from the garden. Upon their entering, Müller closed and locked the door. "You were lucky not to be stopped. You are past curfew. Now, open your jackets further so that I can check your bodies for weapons." Without reply, all three opened their jackets and lifted their arms for the search. Müller nodded and stepped back to examine their faces.

"Now, what do you want of me?"

"This book is why we want to talk to you." Foster took the replica Gutenberg Bible from Gallagher and held the book up to the light. "We know of your fondness for rare books. We believe this item would be desired and well taken care of by you."

Müller stepped back and looked at the Bible.

"If you decide you have no interest in the Gutenberg Bible, we will leave, and you will not see us again. However, if you are interested, we have a deal well worth your time." Foster noted the pause in conversation and handed Müller the Bible.

Müller looked at the book. Foster knew Müller had great interest, and the German's eyes widened like a child entering a candy store. "Come into my library, and let me examine this closer."

Chapter 10
The *Rubáiyát*

The three followed Müller from the entrance to his library. Gallagher was immediately astonished by the great care Müller gave to the room. The library was well kept, and all four walls had bookshelves with perfectly aligned books. Gallagher thought the room might be dusted several times a day, as the polished wooden shelves made the elegantly bound books almost gleam. He was awestruck at the beautiful collection of literary masterpieces.

Müller moved to the front bay window and looked out onto the street. "The Schutzstaffel prefers our citizens keep the curtains open, but we have privacy for a moment."

On the far wall, there was one elaborate oak cabinet with more shelves behind glass doors. Brett walked up to the cabinet. His move was also to scan the back of the room for anyone other than Müller. Seeing no one, Brett viewed the books that lined the shelves behind the glass.

The majority of the books had thick leather bindings trimmed with gold lettering. Looking closely at the titles, he noticed an entire shelf of twenty or so gold-bound books all named *Rubáiyát of Omar Khayyám*.

"Please don't touch." Müller was walking toward Brett. Brett lifted his hands to show Müller he was only looking. Müller moved to a table and placed the Gutenberg Bible on top. He then pulled out a watchmaker's loupe and checked the authenticity of the book through the eyepiece. Turning the Bible over very slowly, he examined the book methodically. "Very precious. Where did you get it?"

"It doesn't matter," Foster said. "I will tell you, though, it is not stolen."

"Hmmm." Müller nodded, still examining the Gutenberg. "Do you also have Volume Two?"

"We only have Volume One," Foster said calmly.

"You mentioned a trade. What do you want of me?"

"A map you made."

"You obviously know me from the university. I have created and own many maps."

"I am looking for a specific map." Foster looked straight into Müller's eyes. "A map that you drew by hand years ago. When you were in East Prussia."

"What are you talking about?"

"You drew two maps of inhabited areas of East Prussia. One had a cave and another a storehouse." Foster looked at Müller's eyes to see if there was any tell. The German remained composed. "We would like the first of the two maps. The map of the storehouse in East Prussia in exchange for the Gutenberg Bible."

"Again, I don't know what you are talking about. I have drawn hundreds of maps."

"This map was one that you drew for Erich Koch. The map was very specific and led to a storehouse where Koch kept items that he … confiscated." Foster was careful not to use the words *stole* or *pillaged*.

Müller's eyes opened when he heard Koch's name and how much knowledge the strangers had regarding Koch's map to his storehouse. He wondered how these three knew of the map. The information was strictly confidential, and few were privileged to that information. At least, Müller believed the information was restricted. "How would you know of this?"

"It's not important," Foster replied. "We simply want map one of two in exchange for the Gutenberg."

"I am sure that if I had such a map, it would not be here."

Foster looked around the room. He was unsure if copies had been made of the second map. "The Bible is yours if you are able to provide us with at least a copy of the map. Are you able to access your maps?"

Looking at the Gutenberg, Müller considered the trade. "If such a map did exist, which I do not believe it does, I might be able to get it for you. Yet you must tell me … how did you learn that I was in East Prussia?" he asked, almost irritated that the information was easily shared.

"It's unimportant. The information was provided by free will. Further, no one knows that we have come here tonight. Neither Koch nor anyone else will know that we were here and made a trade."

"This does not make sense," Müller insisted. "You show up to my home and claim that I made a map for Erich Koch. Somehow you must have gained knowledge that I was in East Prussia with him. But I do not know how you obtained information about the map."

Foster took note of Müller's slip. "We do not want to embarrass Herr Koch nor even make him aware of our conversation. Our goal is to regain items that were taken and placed in that location. In exchange for your cooperation and the map, we have brought you the Gutenberg. These stored items have long been forgotten by Koch and will be unnoticed when we retrieve them."

Müller laughed. "Not by Erich Koch, I can assure you. *Oberpräsident* Koch has not forgotten."

Foster was quick to respond. "He is now in a much different position, and those stored items will not be of any interest to him."

"Not true," Müller said. "Koch remains in East Prussia and may still have a need to store items from our enemies in the Red Army."

"But he will not need your map," Foster said. "Koch is likely unaware that you still have it. Let me stress we only want to make a quiet trade."

"The wealth of this, how do you say, *partial* Gutenberg Bible, would be of no value if I were dead."

Foster's voice was soft, smooth, and persuasive. "You are a wise man, Herr Müller. I wonder if there was something additional that I could offer. If I was able to get you anything you want, would that be something of interest?"

"There is nothing."

From the doorway of the library, a woman's voice said in German, "Who was at the door, Uncle?"

Brett spun around in surprise, as he did not hear someone approach. He saw a young, attractive blonde standing in the doorway. She had curled hair cut just above the shoulders and mesmerizing blue eyes. Brett stared at her.

"*Liebchen*, please, you must not concern yourself with my business."

"But, Uncle," she said in English, suggesting she'd heard the conversation taking place. "I will not let the American greed take your life by trading your cherished map." Müller's niece had been listening to them.

Gallagher walked forward and spoke in German, letting her know they were not a threat. "*Wir meinen es nicht böse, Frau ... ?*"

"*Fraulein*," she retorted. Still in English she added, "My name is *Fraulein* Eva."

"Really!" Gallagher thought of the possible coincidence. "Your last name wouldn't happen to be Braun, would it?"

"Who?"

Foster interrupted. "It's no one, Fraulein. We must continue with our business with your uncle, and we wish you no disturbance. Time is of the essence, and I think we can make a deal to your satisfaction."

"One moment, Eva," Müller said to his niece. He turned to Foster. "Your offer is very precious, but the Gutenberg Bibles are often, how do you say ... a forgery? I would need further time to thoroughly investigate. Therefore, you offer nothing I am interested in. Eva, dear, I will excuse our guests, and we will sit for tea."

"That would be lovely, Uncle," Eva responded with a softness in her voice.

Brett relaxed his body as he stared at Eva. In his relaxation, he leaned back onto the oak cabinet. The cabinet was not braced, and the shelving leaned forward, causing the silver candlesticks that rested atop of the cabinet to fall over, along with the books inside the glass bookshelf.

Eva ran over. "You baboon!" she said angrily. "These are very expensive books, and the slightest damage could destroy their worth."

Brett stood up immediately. "I'm sorry. I didn't mean to cause any damage. Let me help." Brett went to open the cabinet but found the door locked.

"We would not let priceless pieces of art be exposed to your filthy hands," Eva snapped. "Let me do it." She pulled a key from her pocket and opened the door.

"Eva, it was an accident," Müller said to his niece. He then turned to Foster. "Now, I must ask you three to leave."

As Foster nodded and collected the Gutenberg, his mind raced for any alternatives that might entice Müller. He looked to Gallagher, who was watching Brett trying to help Eva with the bookshelf. Brett was using his hands apologetically as Eva picked up the fallen books. Foster focused his eyes past Eva and began scanning the shelves of the cabinet. He noticed the many copies of the *Rubáiyát of Omar Khayyám*.

Foster was vaguely familiar with the book of Persian poetry. Written by an early astronomer and poet, the book had many editions that had value, including those that were encrusted with jewels. "Pardon me, Herr Müller, may I ask why you have so many copies of the *Rubáiyát*?"

Eva stood and was about to answer. "No, my dear, let me answer." Müller smiled and walked over to his bookshelf, motioning Brett away from the shelves. "They are devoted to the single greatest collection of poetry ever written. The collection is entitled *Rubáiyát*. Written by Omar Khayyám over eight hundred years ago, *Rubáiyát* is a collection of philosophical poems that explore our fate and our endless search for meaning in life. The verses encourage us to better understand our life's fleeting nature and the mysteries of our world." Müller's rigid attitude changed. He now had a soft-spoken voice as he described his love of poetry. "Khayyám was amazing, providing meaning to life."

Foster and Gallagher turned to each other. People often sensed when they were about to be lectured to, and Müller was beginning one. Yet Müller's voice was not monotone but oddly calming as he described Khayyám. Eva's anger also dissipated and brought a hint of warmth to her detached coldness as Müller described the author.

Müller returned to Foster, ignoring Gallagher. "Khayyám wrote his poetry in the Islamic Golden Age. No other words I have read … had the words speak to me as much as the *Rubáiyát*. Milton, von Goethe, and even

Shakespeare did not speak the words to me as much as Khayyám. Although there have been many translations from the original Persian language, Edward Fitzgerald did the most impressive translation to English in 1859. His translation introduced *Rubáiyát* to me."

Müller appeared elated as he walked back to the bookcase, smiling toward Eva. Reaching into the cabinet, he lifted one copy of *Rubáiyát* and walked back to Foster. "Look at the detail of this edition. As nearly as impressive as your Gutenberg Bible. The binding of this edition is handcrafted with gold lettering on a leather bind."

"It is indeed beautiful," Foster replied.

"Many editions were handcrafted in similar fashions. Have you heard of the jeweled *Rubáiyát*?"

Foster paused. "Um, no, I have not."

Müller sighed and looked at the book he was holding. "The jeweled *Rubáiyát* is an edition that was far greater than all. The jeweled book was handcrafted and designed by the bookbinder Sangorski & Sutcliffe in 1911. A thousand gems were set in gold, creating an encrusted masterpiece. Beautiful beyond belief." Müller chuckled as his mind became lost in his memories. "As a young copy editor, I had traveled to London many years ago and had the rare pleasure to once see the spectacular jeweled book. I gazed in amazement. The fools. Those foolish fools. Those fools sold the magnificent book for four hundred pounds. Next to nothing. If I had known it would sell next to nothing, I would have done all that I could to collect five hundred pounds and win the bid." Müller shook his head in disgust. "Maybe I was the fool. I was there, and the jeweled *Rubáiyát* could have been mine."

Müller turned away from Foster as rage and regret flushed his cheeks. After a moment, he ran his hands through his graying hair. "I could have had the book. I was so close. I thought the jeweled book would sell for a man's fortune." He took a deep breath to calm his nerves. "You asked what I would do for a trade. The jeweled *Rubáiyát* is the answer. That I would trade for the map you desire. But of course, that is impossible."

Foster would not let that offer go to waste. "Why is that impossible? Where is the jeweled *Rubáiyát*?"

Müller replied harshly, "Undeniably impossible. The jeweled *Rubáiyát* has been lost forever!"

Foster's eyes opened. Finding lost items was his calling. "Lost? Where was the book lost?"

Saddened to share the story, Müller looked to Foster. "The world lost the beauty of the jeweled *Rubáiyát*. A shame, as the book surpassed all others. Gold, jewels, leather-bound, spectacular. A book which took two years in the making. Much rarer than that alleged Gutenberg of yours." Müller stared into Foster's eyes and laughed. "The last time jeweled *Rubáiyát* was seen was in 1912. Unfortunately, the book was lost shortly after and not possible to obtain. Unless you can hold your breath for a long time."

"What do you mean?"

"The famed book sunk aboard one of your allies' ships," Müller answered. "And the ship, along with the jeweled *Rubáiyát*, has never been found."

Foster's thoughts were racing. If the *Rubáiyát* was reported lost on a ship, it might be possible to obtain the book before sinking without disrupting the normal course of history. "Do you mean the book sank aboard an American or British ship?"

"Yes. British ship."

"What was the name of the ship?"

Müller laughed. "Lost at the bottom of the ocean. Have you ever heard of the *Titanic*?"

Gallagher replied without thinking. "The *Titanic* is not lost."

"Of course, it ... unless you Americans have found the ship and kept it secret."

Before Gallagher could reply, Foster put his hand on his shoulder. A solution was forming. "Herr Müller," he began slowly, "the Americans have found the *Titanic*. We were able to raise the waterproof safe which held the book. The jeweled *Rubáiyát* is safe. I am prepared to make a different trade for the map. Because we have possession of the jeweled *Rubáiyát* here in Germany."

Müller nearly spat at Foster. "Hah! Do not insult my love for the art of poetry. It is impossible. The ship sank in the middle of the ocean twenty-five years ago. The undertaking of raising the ship would be massive."

"The ship wasn't brought up," Foster continued with his lie. "Only the waterproof safe that held the *Rubáiyát*."

Müller looked deeply into Foster's eyes.

"We have whetted your appetite with the Gutenberg Bible. Now you know the grand prize for your cooperation. Herr Müller, if we produce the book, could you identify it immediately?"

Müller thought for a moment. "If you really have the jeweled copy of the *Rubáiyát*, then I would unmistakably identify its authenticity."

After a moment of silence, Foster finally said, "We do have the book, and we have it here in Berlin. Nearby." He waited to watch the greed fill Müller's eyes. "Are you prepared to discuss a different trade?"

"Trade for map, do you mean?" Müller queried.

"I can produce the jeweled *Rubáiyát* in exchange for the map to Koch's hidden artifacts in East Prussia. If you agree, I can have the *Rubáiyát* to you in one hour."

Müller impulsively laughed out loud. "I'll make you a counterproposal. I will trade the map you seek if you can bring me the jeweled *Rubáiyát* to me in thirty minutes. But if you fail to return with the book, which I doubt you have, I will call the Schutzstaffel and let them know of your presence."

"Will you have the map in thirty minutes?"

"Yes. I can have the map in that time." Müller smiled. "But only I am able to retrieve the map. And, with the help of my niece, I will also have the proper security measures when you return."

Brett turned to Eva. "What does that mean?"

Eva coldly replied, "It means you will do as my uncle says, or you will not get what you desire."

Foster watched Brett and Eva stare at each other. "Okay, we understand. I accept your deal. The time is now eight twenty-seven. We will return at nine o'clock with the *Rubáiyát*."

Müller looked at the clock on the wall. "If you return by the top of the hour, we will make the trade."

Foster did not hesitate. "Only if there is no police interference. If there are police or military in the area, we will assume you contacted them, and we will leave quickly."

"Then leave the Gutenberg as an earnest gesture. This will also allow more time to examine the Bible closer. During that time, I will contact no one before nine o'clock. This is my word." Müller stared at Foster for a moment before he nodded in agreement.

Foster placed the Bible onto the table in the library. Turning to the door, he motioned to Brett and Gallagher to move. "We will see you in thirty minutes."

As they walked to the door, Müller moved to cut off their exit. "Wait," he said. "This deal was made in haste. I find it difficult to believe you have the *Rubáiyát*."

"Believe what you will. I can produce the book within the time agreed, and I expect you to produce the map." Foster stared deeply into Müller's eyes.

Müller thought for a moment. "If you can provide the *Rubáiyát*, which you cannot, I'll trade the map. However, I say again, do not cross this exchange."

Foster smiled. "Then it's a deal. We will be back here in thirty minutes. You will open the curtains, and you and your niece will remain in the library." Pointing to Brett, Foster said sternly, "My friend will watch you from outside. If there is any intrusion from the authorities, the deal is terminated."

"Windows may not be opened after curfew."

Gallagher was about to question that rule when Eva said, "*Gute Nacht*."

He glanced toward Eva, who had moved to the door without him seeing. Her softness was gone, and she now had a coldness about her. Müller, however, was lusting over the thought of the *Rubáiyát*. He looked again at the clock on the wall. "I will add that if you are not here at our agreed time, I will not hesitate to call the authorities. And believe me, I have that power."

Foster nodded. "Understood."

With no other words, Gallagher, Brett, and Foster left the home through the front door and hastily walked down the street. Passing the buildings next to Müller's house, Foster motioned for the other two to follow him into the back of the dark alley.

Foster pulled out the small return case from his pocket. He locked the latitude and longitude of their location in the alley into the pad. "Okay, I have the coordinates of his alley. We need to find a place to rest and hide out tonight, then in the morning, we return to Munich and then back to our time."

Gallagher turned to Foster. "Foster, what are you thinking? How are we going to get the *Rubáiyát*?"

"Easy. We're going to book passage on the *Titanic* and get that book."

Chapter 11
Fifty-Second Parallel

After Foster locked the fifty-second parallel latitude and longitude coordinates into the return pad, Gallagher looked around the dark alley near Müller's house. He thought of how de-existence occurred when interfering with one's own self. "If we're going to return to this location, we should leave now. Crossing paths with our future selves would be bad."

"Agreed," Foster said. "Let's head south toward the train station and find a park or small forest to hide out in until morning. Then we can return to the portation point in Munich and return home."

The three travelers walked from the alley and onto the street. Staying close to the buildings, they walked in single file and remained in the shadows as they made their way south to seek a quiet place until sunrise. Finding a small park surrounded by a stone wall, the three climbed over the wall and found bushes to hide in and rest for the night. The following morning, they arose early and left the park before sunrise, avoiding any interactions with a park ranger. They boarded a streetcar to the Berlin train station, where Gallagher booked passage back to Munich.

The ease of purchasing tickets and traveling in Germany during 1937 surprised Gallagher. He thought Nazi guards would recognize the American accent and detain or interrogate him and his friends regularly. Yet the three returned to the portation point in the grassy field outside Munich without incident.

Foster opened the small case and used the light on the return pad to position the travelers. Once the return light was solid, he then slid and held the return button to reopen the transport. From their future, the time generator restarted inside the portation room, oscillating its lasers and creating the concentrated beams into the cubic form. Once the time portation was created, the three were encapsulated inside the time cube. The green field where they stood was soon obscured by the gray haze as the travelers felt the sensation of time travel and returned to their own time.

As the gray cube dissipated, the view of the grassy field had changed to the sterile walls of the portation room. The colonel and Maurice were standing at the console. Jumping immediately into conversation, the colonel asked, "How did it go?"

"We met Müller," Foster said, stepping off the portation pad. "He was very observant and noticed us before we arrived. All three of us were able to go inside his home. He invited us into the library."

"Did you offer the Gutenberg?" Maurice asked.

"Müller didn't want to trade the map for the Gutenberg," Foster replied. "He was suspicious the book was a forgery. But he was willing to make a trade for another book."

"Another book," the colonel repeated. "Which book?"

"Before we get into the details, you need to know that someone else was there."

Gallagher added, "His niece was staying with him."

"I don't remember reading anything about a niece," Maurice retorted.

"Neither did we," Foster responded. "There was something guarded about her."

"She was not very welcoming either," Brett added.

The colonel turned to Foster. "It may not matter, since all of you returned. There was no interference. What about the map, Dr. Foster?"

"I'll need a different book, and we'll need to go back to Berlin."

"You want to return to Nazi Germany?" Maurice asked, surprised by Foster's request.

"Yes." Foster handed Maurice the return pad. "I locked the coordinates of an alley nearby his house."

Maurice plugged the return pad into his smartphone. "Yes, you did. You locked the latitude and longitude at the fifty-second parallel."

"I told him I would return in thirty minutes with the other book," Foster added.

Maurice shook his head. "Too many variables to return to Munich. Colonel, if he were to return to Berlin, it may be best to travel north for a portation point to avoid the Munich travel."

"Before I make any judgment," the colonel said, "I need more information on this other book, and I want to hear Dr. Foster's idea in detail."

Foster walked up to the colonel. "We should go to your office. We need to add another trip. There's more than just returning to Germany."

Chapter 12
The *Titanic*

The colonel nodded and moved to her office door. The travelers and Maurice followed without comment. Gallagher knew the colonel was more apt to approve missions when she was at ease in her office. Although she directed all aspects of the PTEUC, the colonel rarely made decisions in areas other than her office. Gallagher believed Foster's request to move the meeting there was to expedite retrieving the *Rubáiyát* and returning to Berlin to trade the book for Müller's map.

Once in the colonel's office and everyone was seated, Foster recapped the details of their meeting with Müller, explaining if the jeweled *Rubáiyát* could be retrieved prior to the *Titanic* sinking, he would be able to successfully trade the book for the map to the Amber Room.

The colonel and Maurice listened intently as Foster shared his idea to return to Berlin shortly after the meeting with the *Rubáiyát* in hand. "I told Müller the waterproof safe aboard the *Titanic* was raised from the bottom of the ocean and we rescued the *Rubáiyát*."

Maurice was glancing at his cell, as he would gather initial information on the *Rubáiyát* and the *Titanic*. "The book was sold at Sotheby's in 1912 for 405 pounds. Much lower than the reserve price, but nevertheless, the book was sold."

Gallagher did the math in his head. "Adjusting for inflation, that amount would be about sixty thousand pounds in today's market."

"Yes and no. The book sold for a low cost, but when you add the *Titanic*, the price is much greater." Maurice placed his cell into his lab coat. "Did Müller believe you had the artifact?"

"I'm not sure. He was apprehensive with the Gutenberg, but his entire mood changed at the possibility of the *Rubáiyát* being recovered. Müller is allowing us thirty minutes to get the book. Hopefully, during that time, he doesn't become cynical." Foster looked at Maurice. "I locked the coordinates for arrival shortly after we left."

"Precision timing will be difficult. You also don't want to arrive and cross paths with yourselves," Maurice interjected.

"Crossing paths won't be an issue," Foster responded. "We moved from Müller's neighborhood last night and camped out in a Berlin park until sunrise. If I'm able to go back and get the *Rubáiyát* from the *Titanic*, I'm positive Müller will make a trade."

"Returning to a sinking ship may not be the best option," the colonel said. "Mr. Maurice, are you able to reproduce the jeweled *Rubáiyát*?"

Maurice paused. "The book itself might be able to be replicated. But I would need time for the gems."

"No, a copy won't work. Müller will know the difference," Foster said boldly. "He nearly spotted the Gutenberg as a fake. An encrusted gemstone replica will never pass. Müller is obsessed with the *Rubáiyát*. He even said he saw the original jeweled book twenty-five years earlier. I need the original."

"The *Titanic* certainly is an event with multiple stories," Maurice interjected. "There are many varying reports of the sinking, and it does make an ideal historical moment to push interference without changing history."

Foster agreed. "I can board the ship and get the book before it sinks."

The colonel was not as confident. "Dr. Foster, that trip would be risky business."

"I'm also considering the pressures of our operation," Foster retorted. "You said the heat is on and our operation is being questioned. It doesn't take much to see that the cost of the PTE complex is huge. We not only have the facility but also three dedicated units."

The colonel considered the outlook of the PTEUC. Pressure had been mounting for months. Being the subject of government funding, leadership often had different thoughts on how best to use funding. A valuable salvage of a lost artifact such as the Amber Room would buy another year, possibly two, in funding.

As the colonel was thinking, Brett raised a finger. "As an alternative, we could return to Berlin moments before the fire breaks out at Müller's house and grab the map before it burns to the ground."

"We don't know where the map is," Foster replied. "Müller has it hidden nearby or somewhere in the house. We could be there for hours looking for the map and still not find it. Also, if I was a no-show by 9:00 p.m., the authorities would be called, and that would also present a problem."

"Interesting," Maurice said. "If the authorities are called, it is possible that the Nazis set the fire to destroy the map and keep Koch from embarrassment."

"The authorities would only be called if I don't return with the book. I have time to return, make the trade with Müller, and leave before the fire. I just need to get the jeweled *Rubáiyát*."

"If you successfully get the book off the *Titanic* ..." The colonel considered the implications. "That artifact would be destroyed in the house fire."

Foster took a deep breath and thought of the repercussions. "The *Rubáiyát* is the key to obtaining the map to the Amber Room. The grand prize, so to speak, is the Amber Room." He turned to Maurice. "Is it worth the sacrifice?"

Maurice looked at the colonel, who said nothing. "The Amber Room is a blend of culture, art, architecture, mystique, and sheer wonder. The *Rubáiyát* is a piece of art and legendary for being on the *Titanic*. But ..."

The colonel did not allow the hesitation. "But what?"

"But ... yes. The Amber Room was a symbol of peace and then stolen by villainy. Two hundred square feet of extraordinary architecture is at least a hundred times more valuable than the jeweled *Rubáiyát*. To rescue the *Rubáiyát* only to lose it in a fire would be tragic. However, if we could unquestionably obtain the map with the book, the loss would be worth the sacrifice to find the Amber Room." Maurice waited to see if the colonel would respond. She did not.

"If Müller does not do the exchange, I'll leave with the *Rubáiyát* and return. That would at least be something."

The colonel agreed. "Yes, that would be something."

"When you meet with the general staff and oversight committee, you will have evidence to support the PTE," Foster pleaded. "At minimum, we will bring you the *Rubáiyát*. At best, we discover the lost Amber Room."

"The Amber Room would be beneficial in our relations with Russia," the colonel said. "Mr. Maurice, what is the survival rate on the *Titanic*?"

Maurice looked at his cell. "Roughly 30 percent chance of survival."

Brett chirped in. "I say we return to Southampton and grab the *Rubáiyát* before the *Titanic* even sails."

"Not a probable option without causing interference," Maurice calmly stated. "The book will be safely stored. Both at the port and on the ship. They will have the crew or security guarding the valuable item. If you want to get that book, you will want to do so when the crew is distracted."

"You mean after it hits the iceberg?" Brett asked.

"Yes," Maurice simply answered. "That ship sank slowly. It took just over two hours to break apart and sink. Less time to board a lifeboat before the passengers knew they were doomed. That gives you about an hour to steal the book without getting caught and board a half-empty lifeboat to avoid missing a launch and drowning or causing an intended survivor not to board and de-existing."

Brett shook his head. "Maybe we should go back to grabbing the map from Müller before the fire starts."

"An hour is enough time," Foster replied. "Right now, time is on our side since we have the coordinates to the alley near Müller's home. We develop a detailed plan to board the *Titanic* and get the book. Maurice, would your team be able to get us the facts of everything that took place during the last hours of the ship?"

"Of course," he said confidently.

Foster held his hands up and smiled. "Great. We use the known details of the ship's last moments to best obtain the *Rubáiyát* in less than an hour and then get off the *Titanic* safely. Once off the ship, we return to Müller's house and make the trade."

The colonel paused as she thought of the many risks involved in Foster's plan. She agreed the knowledge of history was on their side and could be used to their advantage. However, a sinking ship did not offer many alternatives. "I need to consider minimizing the number of travelers placed in danger. I may need to just send Dr. Foster alone."

"Colonel," Brett interjected, "that's a bad idea. All three of us need to go. First, the *Rubáiyát* will be locked into a safe or secure room. I'm the only one that could pick those locks in a short amount of time."

Gallagher added. "The *Titanic* is also a large ship. I'll be able to review the schematics and deck plans. That information is essential. And, as Maurice said, we need to be sure we are receiving the correct map from Müller. I know cartography, and I know Müller's work. I'll know if the map is genuine."

The colonel looked at Gallagher and Brett with a look of seriousness. "You two know the risks. This mission could have you dying aboard a sinking ship. Or being shot in Nazi Germany. Or … de-existing."

"That's not going to happen this time." Gallagher and Brett turned to each other and then back to the colonel. "That's why we need to be a team."

After a silent pause, Maurice looked at the global map displayed on the computer screen. "If the time-generator is transported to a more northern location near the fifty-second parallel, you could portate to both London and Berlin directly."

The colonel spoke without looking toward Maurice. "My preference is to remain at the complex. Transporting the device causes logistical problems."

"Is there a problem with the PTE cargo truck?" Foster asked.

"The truck is fine, Mr. Foster," the colonel retorted. "I am more concerned with a continual and secured energy source to maintain a constant channel for time transmission when you and your team are ready to return."

Maurice was tracing the map. "From the forty-seventh parallel, travel from Munich to London in 1912 will likely be by train, then ferry.

Probably Calais to Dover. Then return to Munich and be re-portated back here and then again to Munich in 1937."

The colonel looked at each member and then at Maurice. She finally held her hand toward the computer screen. Maurice instinctively sat at the computer. "Bring up Berlin, and let's look along the fifty-second parallel. The options are to either return to Munich and travel north or go mobile and relocate to the fifty-second."

On the screen, a red line highlighted the fifty-second parallel over the global map. Maurice described the path. "Following western from Berlin, the line crosses England over the Atlantic Ocean and through Canada."

The colonel pointed at North America on the map. "We have a shared Canadian base just outside of Edmonton, Alberta, which is along the fifty-second."

"An ideal place for an uninterrupted stream of power," Foster added.

The colonel was nodding in approval. "Where in England is the fifty-second parallel?"

Maurice keyed in information into the global map. "The *Titanic* sailed from Southampton, England, which is located at the fiftieth parallel. The northern side of London is at the fifty-second, but a congested area."

"Go more northerly in England to avoid the higher population," the colonel added.

Maurice clicked the computer. "Wait a minute … the *Titanic* departed Southampton on April 10, 1912. The following day, the ship had a brief stop at the port near Cork, Ireland. The fifty-second parallel is just north of that location."

The colonel nodded. "Ireland was predominantly rural. That location will place you closer to the port than in England."

Crossing his finger along the screen, Maurice followed the fifty-second parallel across the globe. "Edmonton, Cork, and Berlin all have similar lines of latitude. We could create a portation point in Edmonton and position your arrival in Ireland on the day the *Titanic* arrives. From the portation arrival point, you will have a short distance south to the port, named Queenstown in 1912."

"What time of day will we arrive in Ireland?" Gallagher asked.

Maurice grabbed the lapels of his jacket. "We would set the coordinates for you to arrive north of Cork just after sunrise on April 11. The *Titanic* arrives and departs Ireland on that day."

"How far north?"

Entering the coordinates from the alley outside Müller's home, Maurice placed a marker on a map of Ireland. "4.825 miles north of Cork is a pasture. You will arrive at the fifty-second parallel portation point that matches the alleyway near Müller's home. From the arrival point, you will need to either walk or find transportation to Queenstown. Once there, you will be able to secure passage in a third-class cabin at the terminal. There will be tickets available for purchase at the port."

"April 11. Four days before the ship will sink in the North Atlantic Ocean," Gallagher added.

Maurice nodded. "Yes. Third-class immigrant tickets will be available the same day as sailing."

Foster nodded in agreement. He looked at Gallagher and Brett, who were also nodding. "We understand. We board the ship in Ireland."

Maurice brought up a new screen on the computer showing a photograph of a different ship than the *Titanic*. "Assuming you are able to obtain the *Rubáiyát* and board a lifeboat, you will be rescued by the *Carpathia*. That ship will sail to Pier 59 in New York City, which is near the fortieth parallel. We will have you locked in at the fifty-second parallel for transport to Berlin. You will need to travel a great deal north from New York to get to the portation point."

The colonel thought for a moment. "In 1912, there were limited options for you to travel north into Canada."

Foster waved off the concern. "We could return to Ireland by booking a return passage on another ship. Ships go to and from Europe on a regular basis."

"Is there any difficulty in obtaining passage back to Ireland aboard a ship, Mr. Maurice?" the colonel asked.

"None, Colonel." Maurice clicked on the screen bringing up a list of 1912 New York to Ireland shipping schedules. "Ships departing the United States were not as full of passengers as those arriving. Booking passage will not be difficult. There are a few options for a returning ship."

"Could we sail New York to Germany?" Gallagher asked.

"Germany might add unnecessary attention. As well as having the book in your possession," the colonel replied. "Return to Ireland. What are the options, Mr. Maurice?"

Maurice continued to scroll through the information on the screen. "One ship you could board is the *Errant*. The route is similar to the *Titanic*—you depart New York and will be able to disembark in Ireland. The return-portation in Cork will be set at the same longitude as the Berlin alley. From Cork, you travel forward in time and arrive in the alley by Müller's house. You will arrive one hour after your previous selves left the area."

"It has to be less than an hour," Foster insisted. "I told Müller I would be there in thirty minutes."

"I'll adjust the return as close as possible. But I want to ensure it is after the last time you were at Müller's house to avoid crossing paths with your previous selves."

"Very well. I am approving the mission. Since our real-time is limited, I would like a precise travel plan timeline."

"Twenty-four hours," Maurice immediately responded.

Foster looked at Maurice and then back to the colonel. "We will be ready in twenty-four hours."

The colonel placed her hands on her desk, indicating the meeting was ending. "I will phone transport and have the time generator disassembled and relocated to Canada in the PTE cargo truck. Maurice, get your team up to speed on the *Titanic* and details on Müller's niece."

Maurice stood. "I'll get the team moving to review specifics and begin preparing supplies for the mission."

The colonel nodded to Maurice, and he exited. She then pulled out her cell and called a preset number. Turning away from the three travelers, she began giving orders to transport the time-travel console and equipment into the specially made PTE cargo truck. The modified semi-trailer had large industrial batteries, which provided a self-contained area to generate a time transport with a specially mounted cabin to allow the PTE-assigned military team to ensure successful transportation into Canada.

Finishing the call, she turned back to the three travelers. "We are in motion to have the console transported into Canada. I will have Mr. Maurice and the research team send period clothing to you first thing tomorrow morning. For tonight, begin reviewing the details of the *Titanic*. We will meet at 0700 hours in the library to review the mission."

Chapter 13
Preparation

The following morning, Foster, Gallagher, and Brett awoke to the delivery of the period clothing by an unnamed member of the military unit. Gallagher was lying in his bed when the clothes were delivered. Although he heard the PTE crew dropping off the clothing, he remained in bed thinking about the *Titanic*. He conceptualized the ship into three different parts: the forward, the mid, and the rear of the ship. He imagined himself walking through the ship to each deck and visualizing the early twentieth-century luxury liner.

Hearing the other travelers talking in the reception lounge, Gallagher dressed in his period clothing. To their credit, Maurice and his team were exceptional at providing well-fitting clothes. He wore a sweater vest with a white shirt and tie and brown shoes. Putting on his brown overcoat, Gallagher walked from his quarters to meet Foster and Brett in the lounge. Foster was dressed in a basic brown jacket and vest with matching pants and wore black heeled shoes. As before, he also wore a brown coat. Gallagher wondered if it was the same jacket or a different overcoat. Brett was the most casual. He wore black laced boots with a white shirt with black pants held up with suspenders, along with a familiar black overcoat.

Foster and Brett nodded in approval as Gallagher displayed his outfit. Satisfied with their period clothing, the three made their way to the library. As was her tradition, the colonel was already there along with Maurice. Maurice looked exhausted, as though he'd been up the entire night. Gallagher would not be surprised to learn that Maurice required his entire team to work through the night preparing for their upcoming mission.

Similar to their trip to Germany, Maurice placed the travel equipment on top of the long library table to review each item. "Good morning, team," the colonel greeted. She walked up to each traveler to review their clothing. "Mr. Maurice, the clothing looks good. Do you have any concerns?"

Maurice shook his head. "My team double-checked the outfits before they were sent to the quarters, and the clothing is appropriate for 1912. We have also repackaged the 1937 outfits and placed them in a waterproof satchel." Maurice pointed to the satchel on the table and looked at Foster. "Upon arriving in Cork, find a location to hide the satchel and retrieve before traveling to 1937. You need to have the same clothes on when you meet Müller."

Foster nodded.

The colonel continued. "Then we are ready to review the primary mission. Let's move into reviewing the items needed to secure the artifact." As was the colonel's preference, mission items were to be referred to as an "artifact." The jeweled *Rubáiyát* now bore that name.

The three walked closer to the table, where Maurice stood at one end. The colonel motioned for Maurice to begin. Maurice strolled to one end of the table and back, looking over the items before describing them to the travelers. He waved his hands over the table as a magician would do when performing an illusion.

"Your mission items will be necessary to successfully travel aboard the *Titanic*, obtain the artifact before the ship sinks, and return to Berlin." Maurice moved to the beginning of the table and lifted three folded binders. "First are your travel documents. Within the binders are your aliases that you will use to book passage in Ireland. When you purchase the tickets, be sure to write your name as initials only or as ineligible as possible. Following the sinking, your names will be listed as unknown due to lack of information or illegible writing. Nevertheless, be sure to review closely so that you're comfortable with the names. The back story is superficial, as you will be posing as immigrants moving to America. Your occupation is laborer."

Maurice placed the travel documents back on the table and then held up a tan canvas bag. "This next item is important. It is a modified canvas bag that is lined with a waterproof rubber bladder. The bladder is identical to those found in waterproof bags from the early twentieth century. The artifact should fit into the bladder without a problem."

"Where is, um, the artifact located on the ship?" Brett asked.

Although premature in the presentation to ask questions, Maurice looked at the colonel, who nodded her head to answer the question. Maurice walked over to a monitor and pulled up a diagram of the *Titanic*. "According to the ship's manifest, the cargo stowage plan shows that books were stored in the stern. Within this storage area, there will be a locked cage. Inside the cage is where the artifact is believed to be stored."

"Is that a definite?" Brett pressed.

"Not definitively. It is possible there is a safe in the cargo hold as well. Unfortunately, the location of the cargo hold was in the stern, which imploded upon sinking. Salvage crews were unable to access the area."

Gallagher moved closer to the monitor, looking at the schematic. "How big is the book?"

"The book is sixteen inches by thirteen inches, and the width with its jewels is estimated at six inches. It will be a tight fit into the bladder, but it will fit."

"As long as it is stored in that cargo hold," Brett added.

Maurice interjected, "The location of the cargo hold may work to your advantage. The iceberg will hit toward the bow. The crew and officers will all be busy attending to the flood of water entering the hull. The cargo hold should be easily accessible. You enter the locked cargo hold, open the cage or safe, and place the book into the waterproof bag."

Gallagher used his finger to follow from the cargo deck to the top deck of the ship. "We'll need to get back to the lifeboat deck after obtaining the book ... I mean artifact. This aft stairwell may work best."

Maurice placed the canvas bag around his head, onto his shoulder, and continued describing the items. "We've doubled the stitching so the strap will not tear as you move quickly to the top of the ship."

Replacing the canvas bag back on the table, Maurice pointed to the additional folded clothes and personal items. "Along with Irish banknotes, US paper money, and additional Reichsmarks, we've also included extra clothing and a basic flint lighter for each of you, as well as inexpensive wristwatches from the turn of the century. These eyeglasses have darkened lenses. They are not reflective lenses but dark enough to hide your eyes."

"The sunny North Atlantic," quipped Brett.

Maurice looked down at the sunglasses. "If you need to look around inconspicuously, no one will be able to see your eyes."

The colonel added, "If you use the sunglasses to scan an area, try not to move your neck, but look out the corner of your eyes."

Maurice then showed the three travelers their hygiene items. The items were time-period appropriate, including toothbrushes, combs, and deodorant. He then picked up a large jar and unscrewed the lid. Inside the jar was a light-yellow waxy substance. "We've included this jar of lanolin."

"Why lanolin?" Brett asked.

Maurice did not answer but looked at the colonel, who turned to Brett. "If you end up in the ocean, you'll want to cover as much of your body as possible with lanolin before entering the water. That water is going to be around thirty degrees, so you won't last long. The lanolin will slow down hypothermia and keep your body heat for an extended time."

"How long?"

The colonel said stoically, "No more than five minutes."

Brett nodded.

"Brett, here are your lock-picking items." Maurice handed him a purse-sized leather bag. "Your tools are inside. They are a combination of Victorian-era lockpicks and early twentieth-century tools." Maurice placed the bag on the table and picked up the older-looking small flashlight. "The next item is a replica of a 1910 Japanese flashlight we designed a while back. The size is ideal if you want to hide it in your pocket." He opened its back and slid out the batteries. "This was the smallest flashlight of the time and used large D batteries. We have replaced the alkaline batteries with upgraded lithium batteries. These two batteries have four times as much power as regular Ds. The modified flashlight also provides twelve volts rather than three. It will generate at least five hundred watts."

"What will we need with all that power?"

Maurice smiled but did not respond. The colonel picked up the hand drill from the table and removed the hand crank. "This drill is ingenious if the artifact is located within a safe. The wooden crank had a standard metal drill bit. Since the drill is made from wood, you may simply drop into the ocean after use. The wood will dissolve in seawater long before the *Titanic* is found in 1985. However, the tip of the drill has been modified with a diamond-core tip. You can see where the cold weld occurred on the bit." She pointed to a small line between the drill and the tip. The silver colors looked continuous, but there was a thin line that divided the two.

Maurice nodded. "The diamond bit will be very helpful for weak-point drilling on a nineteenth-century safe."

Brett added, "If the artifact is not in a locked cage, I'm not sure I'll have enough time to drill the safe by hand cranking."

The colonel turned the hand drill around. "You won't need to. There is more the drill does." She handed it to Maurice.

Maurice clicked a small latch on the hand crank and removed the backing counterclockwise. He removed the spindle crank from the drill's mounting and showed two metal connectors. "These two connectors on the drill are connected to the back of the flashlight. The male-female connection creates twelve volts to power the drill." Placing the back end of the flashlight into the open hand crank, Maurice latched the two together. He turned the on switch, and the drill spun on its own.

"Brilliant," Brett said, smiling.

Maurice unfastened the flashlight and reassembled the drill. He placed both items back on the table. He then unrolled a small sheet of butcher's paper with two visco fuses. "These are basic black-powder fuses. As you each have a flint lighter, any of you can light a fuse."

"There are only two fuses," Gallagher observed. "Which of us won't have a fuse?"

"To minimize interference, Brett will carry both fuses."

"Why am I carrying two fuses?" Brett asked, almost sarcastically.

Maurice turned to the colonel.

The colonel opened a small box lined in plastic wrap and pulled out two cubes of clay. Holding one in each hand, she moved to Foster then handed him one of the cubes. "This is two ounces of C-4 explosive clay, which Foster will carry. Since C-4 will not be invented for another fifty years, you need to keep the fuses separate from Foster. If you're caught, that will increase the odds of the C-4 being mistaken for modeling clay."

"I don't think we'll need the C-4," Brett said. "If I drill the safe, I'm sure I can pick it."

"If the artifact is in a locked cage, you won't need the C-4. Throw it into the ocean once you have the artifact. The salt water will dissolve it. Most of the items you're bringing on the mission can be thrown overboard or sink with the ship. There is minimal interference with history," the colonel added, walking away from the table to the counter. "Please load your items."

Maurice pointed to three duffel bags. "You may load the items, keeping the drill, locksmith tools, and flashlight in separate bags. Once aboard, you're welcome to condense the safecracking tools into one bag."

The three moved to the duffel bags and put the items inside except for the C-4 and the fuses. Gallagher, who was standing next to Foster, saw him place the C-4 in an upper pocket, while Brett tore the butcher's paper in half. He wrapped and placed one fuse in his left pants pocket and another in his right pocket. Once the travel bags were packed, the three travelers stood back from the table.

"Now for the risky piece." The colonel crossed the room to the wall counter and picked up a small black case. She walked to Foster and opened the case to reveal a small pistol-shaped gun. On each side of the gun were cylindrical tubes that ran along the barrel.

"What is it?"

"That is a stun gun," Maurice answered without waiting for the colonel's approval. "The device shoots an ion projectile. When it strikes a person over their clothing, the projectile delivers an electric shock and should leave them incapacitated. If there is a strike on bare skin, it should knock the person out for a few minutes."

The colonel lifted and turned the stun gun, showing Foster how to use the weapon. "Shoot by squeezing this trigger. If you miss, just squeeze the trigger again, but you only have two shots."

Brett was familiar with the defense weapon. "A weapon is way too risky to bring. Stun guns were not invented in 1912. The C-4 is risky, but a stun gun with electric prongs that penetrates the skin …"

"You are partially correct. Electricity existed in 1912, as did handguns. Yet, this stun gun does not use prongs. The ionized projectile will fragment after being discharged, leaving no trace evidence. Further, the trigger uses elastic energy, like a slingshot—a nonmechanical projectile system." The colonel returned the stun gun to the box. "If you're in an interference situation, discharge the projectiles into a wall, the ground, or the ocean, somewhere other than a person. The risk is minimal."

"Knocking out someone could inadvertently cause that person to drown," Gallagher said.

"Unfortunately," the colonel began coldly, "you cannot cause anyone's death, as you know. If you need to incapacitate a person, one of two things will occur. One, you will stun the person and continue with the mission. Or two, you will de-exist, and the weapon will not shoot." "Too risky," Brett said again.

"It's only a 'just in case.' Over half the passengers and crew perish. If someone absolutely needs to be neutralized for you to get the artifact or get off that ship, you will need the stun gun. You have a fifty-fifty chance of causing interference but a greater chance of going down with the ship if you are unable to board a lifeboat."

"We understand the odds. Hopefully, we won't have to stun anyone," Foster said flatly.

"There is also a risk of being separated," the colonel began. "If separated aboard that ship, do not search out each other. There is limited time for boarding a lifeboat. Your primary mission is to obtain the artifact and to seek safe passage onto an early lifeboat, regardless of being together or separated. If you are unable to obtain the artifact within an hour, your secondary mission is to abandon the artifact, board a lifeboat, and return to the PTEUC for plan B."

"What if we bring small radios in the event of being separated?" Gallagher added.

"You will not have enough time to seek each other if separated."

"Plus we have enough modern technology on this mission," Brett added.

"If, for an unknown reason, you are unsuccessful in getting the artifact, return to our time, and we will redeploy to plan B. For now, focus on the primary mission, getting the artifact and offering it to the target in Berlin." The colonel referred to Müller as "the target," similar to the *Rubáiyát* being called "the artifact." She moved to the computer monitor and clicked a photo of the *Titanic*'s boat deck. Tapping the screen with the tip of her fingernail, she turned to the three travelers. "You must get onto a lifeboat. There are no other egress options to avoid sinking with the ship."

"Let's hope it doesn't come to that."

The colonel slid the photo to the side and brought up a visual timeline of the mission. "The PTE cargo truck will arrive tomorrow morning in Canada. That gives you the evening to rest up and review any additional information on the *Titanic* and its schematics. This mission will be much longer than you're used to, since you need to voyage back from

New York to Ireland and then Germany. Yet, since Cork and the Berlin alley are both on the fifty-second parallel, this will streamline the time portation. Once you board the *Titanic*, there's no turning back."

Gallagher seemed preoccupied in his thoughts. The colonel snapped her fingers, and Gallagher looked up. "That ship will sink in the middle of the ocean after departing Ireland. Do you understand?"

Gallagher affirmed.

"Good." The colonel picked up her cell to call her adjunct. She placed the phone down and looked to Foster, then to Gallagher, and finally to Brett. "You are ready to prep for the mission this afternoon and tonight. Keep the outfit you are wearing, as we will have your duffel bags picked up in early morning. We will fly to Edmonton tomorrow at 0500."

A minute after calling, the sergeant was knocking on the colonel's office door.

Chapter 14
Cargo Hold

The three were escorted by the sergeant major back to the travelers unit room to review the mission details. The sergeant excused himself, and the three began reviewing the details of their mission. They worked in the reception lounge, studying their respective aspects and periodically discussing the mission as a group.

Several hours passed, and Gallagher felt comfortable with his responsibilities, particularly the schematics of the *Titanic*'s ten decks. From the bottom stern cargo hold to the forward boat deck, Gallagher estimated eight minutes were needed to climb the aft steps and move forward to board one of the early lifeboat launches. With the additional passengers who would likely crowd the stairwell and boat deck, he added another seven minutes, a total of fifteen minutes to move from the cargo hold to the forward boat deck.

Foster was looking at his computer monitor, studying the details of the jeweled *Rubáiyát*. Brett, however, was fidgeting at his station. A locked cage would be accessible within minutes. However, a safe would require more time. He clicked the stopwatch on the computer and placed his hands over his eyes, imagining the entry into the cargo hold and opening a safe in less than thirty minutes. Shaking his head, he closed the stopwatch and stood up. He paced the rooms for a few minutes before moving back to the computer. On the screen, he brought up information on the *Rubáiyát*.

The ultra-rare copy, lavishly decorated with gems and gold trim, was considered more art than literature. The artist, Francis Sangorski, spent two years finishing it. The jeweled *Rubáiyát* was breathtakingly magnificent, one of the few really priceless valuables that sank aboard the *Titanic*.

Brett stood from his computer screen and began pacing the room again. Finally, he called over to Foster. "Something doesn't make sense." Foster looked up from his computer screen, and Gallagher turned to listen. "I've been thinking about what Maurice said about the artifact ... and where the *Rubáiyát* is located. He said the book was locked in a secured storage cage inside the cargo hold."

"Or safe."

"Why would they place a valuable book in the cargo hold of the ship? If it had that much value, I would think it would be placed in a more secure area over the cargo hold." Brett looked to Gallagher. "According to the cargo stowage that Maurice sent us, the books were stored in the stern of the ship, right?"

Gallagher nodded. "Yes, in the hull of the stern."

"That location is almost as far back on the ship as possible. The opposite end of where the officers were posted. Yet passengers' jewelry and other valuables were kept inside the purser's safe, which is near to the officers in the front of the ship."

Foster tapped his screen. "Maurice and his team used the *Titanic*'s second officer's stowage notes to identify the *Rubáiyát*'s location. Stowage held books, general goods, and even an automobile that was stored in the stern cargo hold."

"Yet the stowage notes do not specify the *Rubáiyát* was stored there," Brett added. "The note by the second officer just added the word 'books.' The *Rubáiyát* was not a common book. I don't see Sotheby's or the owners wanting their irreplaceable, jeweled artwork to be stored with regular books, let alone in the common cargo hold."

"There were other rare books besides the *Rubáiyát* on the *Titanic*," Gallagher added.

"But not jewel encrusted. Those gems alone made the *Rubáiyát* priceless. Far more expensive than other rare books."

Gallagher turned to Foster's monitor. "So, you think it was kept someplace other than the cargo hold?"

"I do. But it wasn't in the purser's safe. His safe was salvaged and brought up from the wreck. The contents did not include the book." Brett thought for a moment. He pointed to Foster's computer screen. "Could you scroll down?" Foster scrolled down to the storage tracking of the *Rubáiyát*. "Where was the book kept before it arrived in Southampton?"

Foster clicked on the tracking logs. The logs prior to the *Titanic* showed the book was stored at Sotheby's in London. The *Rubáiyát* had been recently sold to an American at auction, and Sotheby's arranged the secured shipping of the book to the United States via the *Titanic*. "Look there, it's a bill of lading from London. Sotheby's had the *Rubáiyát* transferred by a private carrier from London to Southampton. The book was then signed over to the Southampton Harbour Company. Could you bring up the company's records?"

"Hold on a minute," Foster said as he clicked on the receipts and records from the company. "Here it is." Foster enlarged an aged receipt. At the top was the heading "THE SOUTHAMPTON HARBOUR COMPANY: 9 APR 1912." The receipt confirmed the company received and secured the *Rubáiyát* from Sotheby's.

"Are there records of the book being transferred from the Harbour Company to the *Titanic*?" Brett asked.

Foster clicked through different receipts and documents. Finally, he stopped on a receipt that indicated a "Sotheby Gemmed Book." The receipt showed a transfer from the Southampton Harbour Company to the RMS *Titanic*, April 8, 1912. The bottom of the receipt listed both Hugh McElroy, chief purser, and William Murdoch, first officer, as signed recipients of the "Gemmed Book." A note at the bottom of the receipt showed the book was to be stored in First Officer Murdoch's safe. The note was signed "H. McElroy, Chief Purser, RMS *Titanic*."

"That's the *Rubáiyát*. It has to be!" Brett exclaimed. "McElroy must have requested Murdoch to lock the book in his safe. The *Rubáiyát* isn't in the cargo hold. It's in the first officer's safe."

"If so, then we almost went to the wrong place." Gallagher frowned. "However, there may be a problem with the first officer's safe. It's in his cabin on the officer's deck. That's a busy location."

Brett was nodding at the new information. "That may work to our favor. Officer Murdoch, as well as the other officers, will be busy after the ship hits the iceberg. It will be nice and quiet in his cabin while I open that safe using the modified drill."

Foster then picked up his cell from the table. "Let's call the colonel and let her know the update."

Chapter 15
Officers' Quarters

After Foster phoned the colonel, she and Maurice arrived promptly in the reception lounge. Foster invited the two to sit next to him. The colonel chose to stand, while Maurice sat at the computer screen next to Foster. Foster updated the two on the discovery of the records tracking the *Rubáiyát* from Sotheby's in London to the Harbour Company in Southampton and then stored in the *Titanic's* first officer's safe.

"Here's the receipt of the *Rubáiyát* being transferred to the first officer and signed off by the purser." Foster had intentionally stopped calling the *Rubáiyát* "the artifact."

The colonel stood and looked at the documents on the screen from over Foster's shoulder. Embarrassed by missing the receipt in his research, Maurice turned to the colonel from his chair. "It appears they are correct, and the book was stored aboard the ship two days prior to departing, not in the cargo but in the first officer's safe."

The colonel did not acknowledge any error and remained focused on the mission. "What additional conditions need to be considered with the new location of the artifact?"

"Hold on," Gallagher interrupted. "Are we rushing this mission?"

The colonel glared at Gallagher. "Mr. Gallagher, how much more time do you need?"

"Well, I'm not sure," he said hesitantly. "It just seems that we missed something here, and we might miss something else."

"That's always a possibility," the colonel retorted. "I will ask you again, Mr. Gallagher. How much more time do *you* need, considering the new conditions?"

"Me?" Gallagher looked at Foster, who looked unaffected by his question. "I don't need additional time. It actually works better for the book to be on the boat deck."

"Good. Does anyone else have additional conditions to consider?"

"The safe is in a cabin on the officers' deck, near the bridge. It'll be a busy area," Gallagher said.

"However, as Gallagher said, we'll be closer to the lifeboats. The officer's deck is in the forward part of the main boat deck." Foster brought up the deck plan on his computer screen.

"The forward lifeboats are nearby and the first to be launched," Gallagher added.

"The location is different," Maurice said, "but after the iceberg, the officers will be ordered to their emergency stations. They won't be in their cabins. The mission items could remain the same."

Brett raised one finger. "If I'm able to get into the first officer's cabin without being seen, I can block the door from the inside to avoid a surprise interruption. In the cargo hold, it did run the risk of crew members interrupting without warning."

The colonel studied the schematic for a moment. "If Foster and Gallagher actively serve as outlooks, Brett would have enough time to enter the cabin and retrieve the book."

"Entering the cabin door will be an easy pick," Brett added to her train of thought. "Breaking into the safe with the modified drill should take no more than fifteen to twenty minutes."

"We shaved fifteen minutes by not having to navigate from the bottom of the ship to an available lifeboat," Gallagher said.

Maurice stood up. "You comfortably have a half an hour before you need to move to and board one of the early lifeboats."

Gallagher thought of the timeline. "Maurice is right about thirty minutes. If Brett has the book in less than that, we'll have no issues boarding the first or second lifeboat launched. Few passengers will be aboard, and we could offer help in rowing."

"No one wanted to leave the comfort of the ship," Maurice added. "The passengers thought the ship was indestructible. Subsequently, or maybe I should say consequently, very few boarded those early lifeboats, and one of those will get us to safety."

Foster stood up from the computer. "Our success will be to move as quickly as possible after the ship hits the iceberg. Brett will need to enter the first officer's cabin moments after that."

The colonel looked pleased. "The mission remains. The new location appears to be an advantage for success." She turned to Maurice, who nodded in approval. "We have a plan. Let's try to get some rest and then meet the colonel at 0500 to fly to Edmonton, where the time generator will be ready to transport you to early morning in Ireland on April 11, 1912."

Brett smiled. "Then we're off for a cruise on the *Titanic*."

No one responded to Brett's attempt at humor. The colonel moved to the door with Maurice following.

That evening, Gallagher rested uneasily. He tossed and turned in his bed. He was not thinking about the *Titanic* but rather about Nazi Germany. There was something that still bothered him about Wolfgang Müller's niece.

Chapter 16
Queenstown, Ireland

Gallagher awoke from a drowsy sleep. He did not remember falling asleep and momentarily lost his sense of time. Brett was calling to him from the reception lounge. "Time to go, Gallagher! You don't want to be late. I'll meet you in the tunnel."

Sitting up on the bed, he looked for his duffel bag, but the PTE support team had already picked it up. *I was deeply asleep*, he thought, having not awoken when the team took the bag.

Gallagher dressed and moved to the reception hall. Brett wasn't there. He walked out into the PTEUC tunnel, where he found Foster, Brett, and the colonel waiting by a gray van to bring them to the airport. In the driver's seat was the sergeant, who had earlier driven him and Brett following the World's Fair mission.

Gallagher boarded the back of the van first, and they rode together to the nearby military airport. The flight to Edmonton lasted just under two hours. While on board the plane, the colonel continued to remind the travelers of the time restraints and need to board a lifeboat prior to the *Titanic* sinking.

Upon arrival at the Edmonton military base, a transport van was waiting to take them to the secured PTE cargo truck. The truck had arrived the evening before, and preparations were complete for the travelers to begin their mission. Gallagher noticed Foster appeared more relaxed than his earlier trip to Germany. Possibly because Ireland did not feel as hostile as Germany, he appeared calm and content.

The team was driven to the PTE truck, parked intentionally in the rear of the base, away from any compound buildings. They boarded the truck with their duffel bags, Gallagher first. He noticed Maurice, who was kneeling behind the console, speaking with an unmarked soldier. Gallagher wondered if Maurice had arrived in Edmonton the night prior.

Maurice stood up to receive the team. "The portation coordinates have been entered into the PTE console, and everything is operating at full capacity."

The three stood inside the trailer and looked at the portation pad, where the array of lasers would create the time displacement. The colonel moved behind the console and looked over Maurice's shoulders onto the monitor.

"We're all set," Maurice said to the colonel. He then turned to the travelers. "Does everyone have their return pad?"

Brett, Foster, and Gallagher all pulled out the metallic return case. Maurice nodded. "Good. Please bring your bags to the portation pad."

Foster led Gallagher and Brett past the array of lasers and placed their duffel bags and the waterproof satchel onto the portation pad. The three remained on the pad. Behind Maurice, the colonel excused the unmarked soldier and followed him to the exit. Once the soldier departed, the colonel secured the door. Turning to Maurice, she said, "We can begin. They're ready."

Maurice entered a few commands into the console keypad. The console began the familiar humming, and the lasers soon generated the cube around the travelers, who were no longer visible to the colonel or Maurice. The three travelers were encapsulated in the time cube and transported back in time from the PTE truck from Edmonton, Canada, to the south of Ireland on April 11, 1912.

The travelers felt the sensation of time travel as the view of metallic walls of the PTE truck's cargo trailer became fogged with a hazy cube. As the haze dissipated, the travelers were standing atop a small hill in southern Ireland. The sloped hill was slippery with wet grass. Looking up, Gallagher could see dawn breaking through a drizzling overcast. *More rain*, he thought.

Foster looked at the time of the return pad and adjusted his wristwatch. "The time is 7:05 a.m." Gallagher and Brett adjusted their watches while Foster watched the rising sun.

Brett looked east and noticed a few cottage homes in the distance. "Should we go east?" he asked, pointing to the sun rising over the white stucco cottages with straw roofs.

Lifting a duffel bag and the waterproof satchel, Foster pointed in a southerly direction. "No, we're heading south. The port is that way. The walk shouldn't be long, but be careful not to slip on the wet grass."

Gallagher lifted his foot and slid the shoe on the grass. "Our shoes seem to be more for ballroom dancing than providing traction."

"Just go easy down the hill," Foster replied. "Once we reach the road, it's going to be an easy walk to the port. Remember to use only our aliases moving forward."

Brett squatted down as he descended the hill, keeping his heels planted firmly on the ground to prevent himself from falling as he shuffled down. Gallagher followed, taking small steps to avoid slipping and having muddy pants for the walk to the port. Foster was the last to make his way down. Once he reached the bottom, Foster pointed toward a patch of three shrubs. "Let's hide the satchel in those shrubs. Three bushes by themselves are an easy reminder of where it's hidden." Foster walked to the shrubs and climbed into the bushes. Gallagher and Brett looked around the countryside for anyone watching, but they were alone. Foster reappeared from the bushes moments later. "Let's find the road and get to the port."

After less than an hour's walk, the three arrived outside Cork at eight. Motioning to a horse-drawn carriage, Foster was able to procure a ride to Queenstown, south of Cork, where the *Titanic* would soon arrive to pick up passengers before traveling across the Atlantic.

Like most port cities during the turn of the century, people arrived by different types of transportation. Some by motorized vehicles, some even by boat. But the majority arrived by horse-drawn carts and stagecoaches. The morning sun was cool and the ocean air brisk as Foster, Gallagher, and Brett reached the Queenstown port. Foster paid the driver with an Irish banknote.

The *Titanic* would arrive within the next few hours, which left limited time to secure passage aboard the vessel. Arriving at the ticketing office, Foster provided the paperwork with the alias names and the money for three third-class tickets. Maurice was correct about the ease in purchasing passage tickets for third-class travel. It was typical for American-bound immigrants to purchase tickets up to the last moment before sailing.

Moving over to the pier, they found a small group of people waiting for the ship to arrive. The time was approaching 10:00 a.m., and the ship was to dock in another ninety minutes. Looking out into the busy ocean bay, Gallagher was momentarily surprised at the number of ships sailing in the harbor. A smoke-filled sky rose above the waters from the many coal engines. Looking past the traffic, he was unable to see the *Titanic* on the horizon.

Foster looked to the rear of the crowd. "Let's move to the back. She'll be here soon, and we should find a quieter place where we can put our bags down and wait." Moving to the rear of the crowd, the three stood by a timber pole and waited for the great luxury liner.

Around 10:30, the group of spectators grew larger. During the next hour, nearly one hundred arrived to watch in awe as the *Titanic* pulled into the harbor. The ship already had a reputation, possibly because she was built in Belfast, and the Irish citizens had a special bond with her. Or possibly because the ship's designer proudly claimed her to be unsinkable. Either way, the crowd amassed to see the ship.

On the horizon, a spectator spotted the ship in the distance. "Here she comes!"

As the ship neared the bay, the majestic beauty of the immense luxury liner caught the attention and amazement of all as tugboats aided the ship into the harbor. The *Titanic* towered above the smaller boats that filled the harbor. The blues of the water, combined with the colors of the sky, lit the ship in an exquisite portrait.

The name *Titanic* was appropriate, given the ship's immense size and beauty. The white deck stood proudly over the black hull of the ship. Barely above the waterline, the red trim of the ship's base cut headstrong into the ocean. The tan-and-black smokestacks topped the ship with splendor. There were no smoke burns on the stacks, revealing how recently the ship was built.

Gallagher stared in amazement. Foster noticed his companion's awestruck admiration. "Don't forget to keep a low profile," he whispered. "Shortly, we have to take a tender out to the ship, so try not to stare too much."

Gallagher glanced around at the spectators all staring out into the harbor as the *Titanic* arrived in Roches Point, Queenstown. He knew no one would question his fascination with the ship, as her beauty spellbound everyone.

Chapter 17
Embarkation

Passing near the Roches Point Lighthouse, the beacon that guided vessels into the port in the night, the *Titanic* sailed into the harbor. The harbor pilot, along with the tugboats, assisted the majestic ship into her berth at the center of the port. From the shore, Gallagher watched two large anchors, one port and one starboard, splash into the water and down to the murky bottom of the bay.

Once secured to prevent drifting, tenders began ferrying passengers from the pier to the ship. Before moving toward the tender entrance, the three travelers waited for the first- and second-class passengers to be ferried first. As the third-class passengers began lining up to be ferried to the ship, Foster motioned to lift the duffel bags and begin moving to the tender entrance. Walking up to the gate, the three travelers showed their boarding passes to the attendant. Waved onto the pier, the three casually entered the waiting area.

Gallagher looked at the group of waiting passengers. There was a family nearby, pointing and smiling. Gallagher heard the mother say, "Isn't the ship ravishing?" He wondered whether the family would survive. Shaking off the thought, he looked at the arriving tender's crew tying a docking line to the pier. After the small wooden boat was tied, a small gangway was lowered from the boat to allow passengers to board. The travelers, along with the other waiting passengers, crossed the gangway and were ferried across the harbor.

As the tender neared the RMS *Titanic*, Gallagher studied the exterior of the immense ship. Having thoroughly studied the deck plans, Gallagher knew they would be boarding the lower E Deck. Other than the main boat deck atop the ship, the decks were alphabetized with A Deck being the highest and G Deck the lowest. Pulling up to the ship, the docking-line rope was secured and the gangway lowered for passengers to board. The tender gangway was attached to a steel-walled entrance, where freshly hammered rivets lined the bulkhead. Gallagher led the boarding, and as he passed the large hatch and entered the ship, it became apparent the splendor of the *Titanic* was found on the upper decks and not at the E-Deck entrance.

Once aboard, a dozen crew members welcomed passengers with their proper British accents. Gallagher declined the assistance from the crew in carrying their duffel bags or finding their stateroom. He continued past the overly polite crew and walked into the E Deck passageway, which ran the length of the ship.

Once in the passageway, Gallagher walked along the wooden floors to the bow, with Foster and Brett following. Over his shoulder, Gallagher called back, "Our stateroom is down one deck. On F Deck."

Finding the stairs, they passed two passengers comfortably laughing while walking up the stairs. The passengers wore casual rugby clothes. "They probably boarded in England," Gallagher whispered.

On the F Deck, Gallagher walked down the passageway, reading the cabin numbers. Once he located their stateroom, he opened the door, and the three travelers looked into their small accommodations. The room was no larger than a public bathroom. On each wall were stacked beds, the frames secured to the walls. Underneath the bottom bed was a drawer to store personal items. On the opposite wall to the entrance, the waterline was visible through the porthole. When all three stood inside, there was little room to move except to exit.

"Where's the bathroom?" Brett asked somewhat jokingly.

Gallagher smiled. "It's a shared system in third class. There is no running water in our cabin, so communal sinks and shared bathrooms."

Brett suddenly had a flashback to his college dormitory, where he shared a bathroom with twenty college freshmen. "On the bright side, we have a cozy cabin."

"That's not all." Gallagher pointed to the porthole. "I don't want to sound pessimistic, but our cabin is on the starboard of the ship. The iceberg hits just below us."

"Great," Brett said sarcastically.

"Don't worry," Foster said as he looked at the ocean through the small porthole. "We won't be in the cabin when we hit the iceberg. Let's just make ourselves comfortable, because we have a few days before *it* happens."

Brett said, "Today is the eleventh. The ship hits the iceberg late evening on the fourteenth and sinks early the fifteenth."

"Yes, three days." Gallagher looked at the bunk beds. "I'll take this top bunk."

"It's all yours," Brett replied, patronizing Gallagher claiming the bunk.

"I'll take a bottom bunk," Foster said, sitting down on the cot. "After we depart and clear Ireland, let's walk the ship and get comfortable with our surroundings. For now, we can relax."

Brett moved to the other lower bunk bed. Lying down, he reached his hand over and tapped the steel hull. "Well … hopefully the iceberg doesn't hit this high."

Chapter 18
Exploring the Ship

In the early afternoon of April 11, 1912, the three travelers heard the *Titanic* raise her two anchors to resume her maiden voyage. As they departed Queenstown, Gallagher peered out the port and watched the rolling hills of the Irish coastline as the harbor pilot guided the grand luxury liner out to sea. Clear of Ireland, the *Titanic* took full command and set sail across the Atlantic bound for New York City, the Irish coast disappearing from the horizon.

Gallagher led Foster and Brett onto the main boat deck. Exiting the stairwell, Gallagher looked up at the smokestacks to get his bearings. "We're in the second-class promenade. We need to move forward past the engineers' promenade and into the first-class promenade. The first-class is adjacent to the officers' promenade, which houses the bridge at the bow."

As the three wandered the boat deck, they would occasionally give a polite nod to the many passengers strolling by. All three shared the same sadness about the passengers, including children, who were unaware of their impending fate. Of the 2,200 passengers and crew, there were only three people aboard the ship who knew the final destination of the RMS *Titanic* would not be New York City.

Brett pointed to a lifeboat secured on the side of the boat deck. "There is our salvation."

Gallagher moved over to one of the double-lined wooden lifeboats, which was securely fastened onto strong steel brackets attached to a crane. After looking over the lifeboat for a few moments, he looked down the deck for any prying eyes.

"What number is this lifeboat?" Foster asked.

Pointing to the first large lifeboat, Gallagher looked to the front of the ship. "We're on the port side, so that is Lifeboat 10." He turned to the lifeboats in front of him. "The first lifeboat in the front of the ship is number 2. As we head down ship, the lifeboats are numbered 2, 4, 6, 8, 10. Behind us are Lifeboats 12 and 14. The last one toward the stern is Lifeboat 16. These mirror the lifeboats on the other side, with the exception of the numbers being odd rather than even." As Gallagher walked along the deck of the ship, he continued to describe the lifeboats.

"Each lifeboat is thirty feet long and holds about sixty-five, sixty passengers and five crew." Walking forward on the deck past the engineers' promenade and into the first-class promenade, there was a break between the fore and aft lifeboats. "These two lifeboats coming up are Number 8 and Number 6. The officers' promenade is just after 6."

Brett looked past Gallagher and examined a covered lifeboat. The boat sat nestled on the crane, waiting for its one mission. "These are pretty small boats," Brett said. "No wonder most people went down with the ship."

"The lifeboats carried about half of the passengers and crew," Gallagher clarified. "But you're right, they are small."

Gallagher led the travelers through the first-class entrance. As the three approached the forward part of the main deck, they reached a restricted area with a sign that read *Crew Only*. "We're at the end of the First-Class Promenade Deck. Past this is the Officers' Deck. That hatchway just past the barrier is where First Officer Murdoch's cabin is located, along with the safe holding the *Rubáiyát*."

"This area isn't difficult to enter at all," Brett said, standing by the gate that divided the first-class and officers' promenade. "Just walk around the barrier."

Gallagher nodded toward a hatch leading to the Officers' Deck. "The hatch leads to the officers' cabins. Murdoch's is the fourth cabin left of the hatchway. The officers' cabins are located near the bridge, to make it easy to move to the wheelhouse. The captain and other officers are also in this area. After the ship hits the iceberg, all the officers will be called to emergency duties. They'll be plenty busy."

Brett nodded. "The busier they are, the better for me. Once I'm outside, we could hop into one of these nearby lifeboats."

"It may be best to go to the other side of the ship to minimize recognition," Foster mused.

"Starboard does have the first lifeboat launched. Lifeboat 7, which is on the other side of the ship, opposite Lifeboat 8." Gallagher pointed to the nearby Lifeboat 8.

Foster nodded. "What's the quickest way to cross the deck?"

Gallagher looked to a hatchway. "Through the first-class entrance."

"Let's take a look at Lifeboat 7."

The three walked through the first-class entrance with its wrought-iron-domed ceiling. The entranceway included seating, a piano, and the top landing of the first-class staircase, which was often called *the Grand Staircase*. Exiting to the starboard side, Gallagher led Foster and Brett to Lifeboat 7, the fourth along the boat deck from the bridge.

Foster raised his arms and pointed from Lifeboat 7 to the first-class entrance. He estimated the time needed to move from the officers' quarters, through the first-class entrance, and reach Lifeboat 7 was less than sixty seconds. "Once you have the book, exit the hatch, and we'll meet at the first-class entrance on the port side. From there, we cross the ship to Lifeboat 7. If separated, we meet here, quickly and quietly. The longer it takes, and the more water that fills the forward compartments, the more difficult it'll be to board Lifeboat 7."

Brett noticed four smaller boats anchored atop the roof of the officers' quarters. "What about those smaller lifeboats? Maybe those are the best bet to board."

"Those are collapsible A through D," Gallagher said. "The collapsible lifeboats won't be an option. They were considered 'man-overboard' boats and will be launched last. By the time they're launched, passengers know the ship is going down. Sadly, only two of the four collapsibles held passengers. The other two were cast into the ocean and drifted away before passengers could get aboard."

"Oh, my," Brett simply said.

Gallagher motioned overboard. "The collision will happen below here at 11:40 p.m. this Sunday. The ship will turn to avoid a direct impact. The iceberg will tear open several holes along the starboard side, just below the waterline. Those holes, combined with the frozen water, will cause the plates of the hull to buckle inward and flood the forward part of the ship."

"Just below Lifeboat 7?"

"Yes. The tear begins close to the bow and continues through five, possibly six, of the *Titanic*'s fifteen watertight compartments."

Foster looked at the lifeboats lining the side of the main boat deck. "What time does the lifeboat begin lowering?"

"They begin preparing Lifeboat 7 just after midnight," Gallagher said. "Captain Smith is told the ship will not stay afloat. Knowing the inevitable, he calls the order to abandon ship. At about twenty-five minutes past midnight, Number 7 is lowered at slightly less than half capacity."

"Brett, you have no more than forty minutes to get in and out of the cabin." Foster tapped the wood hull of Lifeboat 7. "Our prime time to board Lifeboat 7 will be shortly after the captain calls 'abandon ship.'"

"As the forward compartments take on water, the bow sinks deeper and deeper, and the ship will list. When you feel the ship listing, you know time is running out."

Gallagher pointed to three lifeboats forward of Lifeboat 7. "Since the passengers will be unaware the ship will sink, the early lifeboats will carry less than capacity. Lifeboat 1 is the most forward and is hanging over more than the other because it's smaller than Lifeboat 5 and Lifeboat 3. There is room on all three lifeboats, but I would recommend Lifeboat 3 or 5 because they have more capacity and may be easier to board. After those three are launched, passengers will fill the remaining lifeboats to capacity. I think it'll be next to impossible for three men to board a lifeboat."

"The unsinkable will sink," Brett sighed.

"Right. The later lifeboats will be overcrowded and limited to only women and children. The passengers begin to realize what the captain already knows ... the *Titanic* will sink. The ship will eventually dip so far into the ocean that the spinning propellers are lifted out of the water. The downward angle is so great that it causes everything to crash forward to the bow, including the giant boilers. When that happens, the electricity goes out and the ship is left in darkness as it continues sinking."

"That'll be horrifying," Brett said, thinking of the many lives that would soon perish.

Gallagher continued grimly. "The survivors in the lifeboats will be in darkness. They won't be able to see the sinking very well, but they will hear the steel hull break in two when the weight of the stern tears it from the bow." Using his open hands, he created a ninety-degree angle. "The bow will submerge into the ocean, still attached at the keel with the stern. The stern will balance out and appear to float out the disaster. Unfortunately, the weight of the submerged bow finally rips free of the stern and goes down. The stern, which is filled with air, spins around and sinks vertically. When water pressure overcomes the pressure of the trapped air, the stern implodes, nearly destroying the rear part of the ship before reaching the bottom of the ocean."

"Along with fifteen hundred souls aboard." Foster sighed at the forthcoming catastrophe. "We'll need to be as quick as possible to escape."

"We'll be good with time," Brett began confidently. "The ship hits the iceberg at 11:40 p.m. We need to be by the port-side officers' promenade by 11:35. I'll be ready to enter the first officer's cabin. If all goes well, I'll be out by midnight. If things are going slower than expected, I'll abandon the mission at 12:15."

While the three were standing in front of Lifeboat 7, a group of passengers walked nearby, glancing toward them. Foster was growing uneasy standing still out in public view. "We need to move from here. Let's head to our stateroom and stay low for the next few days."

Gallagher realized they hadn't eaten that morning. "First, we should go by the galley and get some food and water."

"Good idea. Lead the way."

Gallagher led the travelers back to the stairwell and to the third-class dining saloon, where they were able to eat a late lunch. While eating, Gallagher and Brett both took extra bread to bring back to the room.

Chapter 19
Day Two

As the *Titanic* sailed the first evening in the cold waters of the North Atlantic, Foster and Brett slept through most of the night and well into Friday morning. Gallagher caught only a few hours of sleep. Lying in the small stateroom, his mind raced through the mission to avoid boredom from overtaking him. There was an element of sadness that the *Rubáiyát* was to be destroyed in Müller's house fire. But he knew the *Rubáiyát* would work in a trade for the map. Gallagher believed that sailing aboard the *Titanic* and stealing the famed *Rubáiyát* was the best solution.

On the second day, the travelers began preparing and organizing the mission items. Each of the duffel bags was emptied onto a lower bunk. Foster did an inventory of the items: flashlight, hand drill, three life vests, lanolin, and lock-picking tools. After review, the mission items were placed into one bag. On top of the items, three life vests were placed in the bag and the clasp snapped shut. The only items not placed in the bag were the stun gun, the C-4, and the two fuses, which Brett and Foster kept in their respective pockets.

"We're all set," said Gallagher.

"Hopefully," Brett replied.

"What do you mean 'hopefully'?" Gallagher asked. "Are you second-guessing the book's location? Could that book be in the cargo?"

"No, I don't think it's stored down below." Brett stood and looked out the port window. "But we're basing the location on the receipt we found in the archive."

"The receipt showed the purser placed the *Rubáiyát* in Murdoch's safe."

Brett turned around. "I know, and I believe it's here."

Gallagher almost laughed out loud. "If it's not in that safe, then this voyage may be a waste of time."

"I'm sure we haven't wasted time," Brett replied confidently. "The book being located in a separate location from the cargo makes sense. It's too valuable an item. Sotheby's or the owner likely specified the book to be secured to ensure there was no risk of loss. The cargo hold has far too much traffic, and the purser's safe is opened and closed throughout the voyage. It makes sense why the first officer had it in his safe."

"If it was that important, could it be in the captain's safe?" Gallagher asked.

"The captain would have been too occupied to be concerned about the safety of a book. The first officer's safe makes sense."

"What if it's not there?" Gallagher continued pessimistically.

"I'm counting on it being here. But I suppose if worse comes to worst, and it's not in Murdoch's safe, I might be able to make it to the captain's safe."

"We're starting to get stir crazy locked in this tiny stateroom," Foster said, shaking his head. "There isn't enough time to start second-guessing. We have to believe the book is in Murdoch's safe. If it's not, we abandon the mission, get on a lifeboat, and return to the PTEUC for plan B. But let's not get distracted with unnecessary thoughts and stray from our current plan."

"The colonel's plan about storming Müller's house is not the best idea," Gallagher said.

"Neither is going down with this ship," Foster insisted. "We're going to remain focused on the first officer's cabin. For now, we wait."

Chapter 20
Last Day

The travelers' fourth and final day of the voyage, Sunday, April 14, finally arrived. The three ate their meals in the stateroom, keeping unseen from the other passengers and crew until nightfall. Restlessness was taking over as evening arrived. Gallagher watched as Foster sat in the middle of the bed and folded his brown wool blanket. The limited amount of space within the stateroom did not allow Foster to make perfect folds. He finished and placed the blanket at the foot of the bed.

"We're getting nearer to the iceberg," Gallagher said.

Foster checked his watch. "At 10:00 p.m., we can head up top and walk around the main deck to double-check the distance from the officers' promenade to the early lifeboats. I want to time the distance to each lifeboat as they're launched. If we're not able to board Lifeboat 7, we need to know how long it takes to move to the next lifeboat down the line or on the opposite side of the ship. We have to be aboard one of them without exception … even if separated."

Gallagher glanced at his watch. "It's 9:55."

"If we head up to the deck now, we have about ninety minutes before we need to get into position on the forward deck," Brett said.

Foster stood and picked up the folded blanket from his cot. "Also, let's take our blankets from the bed and store them somewhere on the boat deck."

"Why?"

"Possibly use them for extra warmth while on the lifeboat. Fold your blankets, and I'll carry them." Foster peered out the porthole as Brett and Gallagher folded their blankets and placed them at the foot of his bed. Glancing again at his watch, Foster scanned the stateroom. "It's time."

Just after 10:00, the three travelers put on their coats. Brett lifted the duffel bag with the mission items and life vests onto his shoulders. The life vest had six cork floatation blocks on each side with two straps. Foster placed the three folded blankets under this arm and moved to the door. Gallagher and Brett both nodded, and Foster opened the door, and the travelers left their stateroom for the last time. The two other travel bags, along with the extra clothes and hygiene materials, were left behind to sink with the ship.

Once in the passageway, the three walked down the third-class deck toward the stairs. Passing the mailroom, they ascended the stairs near the swimming pool. Passing the connecting decks, they walked through a first-class passageway and came upon the first-class staircase. The three stood at the bottom of the steps, gazing up at the glass dome above. During the day, sunlight would create a picturesque mosaic of lights on the staircase.

The sight of the wooden, hand-carved staircase was breathtaking. At the bottom of the steps stood the statue of a child holding a lamp. Gallagher walked over to the statue and touched the piece of work. "They brought that to the surface," he said.

Gallagher moved to the middle landing of the stairs to admire the clock. On each side of the clock, two angels seemed to guard the time, which read 10:15. The landing of the Grand Staircase was one of the iconic memories of the ship. Time did not allow Gallagher to take in the moment as Brett and Foster continued up the stairs. Gallagher followed to the top, which exited onto the main boat deck.

After they reached the first-class entrance at the top of the stairs, lifeboats were visible through the windows on the starboard and port sides of the ship. Walking out the starboard doors, a few passengers sauntered in the brisk evening. The three walked across the deck to Lifeboat 7, which hung from the roped cables attached to the davit crane.

"Let's start from here and walk to the back of the ship and cross to the port side." Foster pointed toward the front of the ship. "Then walk up to the officers' promenade."

The three made their way around the boat deck. Walking from the forward first-class promenade, they crossed the engineers' promenade and into the second-class promenade. Passing the four distinctive smokestacks, the travelers reached the stern of the ship. The three paused at the furthest aft point and looked into the black void of the dark ocean. From the stern, the aft lifeboats were noticeable. Without saying a word, the three shared the somber moment.

Foster rounded the stern of the ship onto the port side. Brett and Gallagher followed as the three made their way to the front of the ship. Passengers, in both the second- and first-class promenades, passed the travelers, some occasionally giving a pleasant nod to the three.

As they neared the officers' promenade, Gallagher pointed toward the bridge, where a yellow light was above the bridge cab. "The room with the yellow light is the wheelhouse, which is adjacent to the officers' quarters passageway."

"Is the passageway visible from the wheelhouse?"

"No, the quarters are separated by a door."

Foster nodded and spoke to Brett adamantly. "If the wheelhouse door is open, turn around. The officers might see you in the passageway."

"If that passageway is empty, I could pick Murdoch's door in seconds and be in the cabin moments after the ship hits the iceberg." Brett hoped to be on the main boat deck when Captain Smith ordered the evacuation. He looked toward the hatch that led into the interior passageway of the officers' quarters. "Once inside, opening the safe will take no more than twenty minutes."

A ship's steward was walking toward them along the officers' promenade. "Come on," Foster whispered. "Let's go before we cause any suspicion." Turning the corner, the three walked toward the port side of the deck.

Along the deck, they passed stacked sundeck chairs resting against the bulkhead. "Before we begin, I'll put the blankets under these." Foster took the three blankets and jammed them between two of the lower chairs. Looking at his watch, the hour passed 11:00 p.m., and they were now about a half hour from the collision. "Let's do one more loop around the boat deck. By the time we return, we'll be close to the iceberg."

"We could walk down to A Deck to warm up," Gallagher suggested.

"Let's stay outside to minimize interactions with passengers. Plus, we can get accustomed to the cold." After circling the ship, the three returned to the forward part of the first-class promenade, near the restricted area of the officers' promenade. Brett placed the duffel bag on the deck and knelt. He opened the bag and handed Gallagher and Foster their life vests. He then moved his to the side to see the flashlight, hand drill, and lock-picking tools. Brett looked up and gave a thumbs-up to Gallagher and Foster.

Tapping his pockets, Foster felt the C-4 and returned the thumbs-up. Gallagher looked up and down the ship and raised his thumb. Snapping the clasp on the duffel bag, Brett lifted the strap onto his shoulders. "I'm set."

Foster nodded. "Remember to put your life vest on before you leave the first officer's cabin."

"I will."

Foster nodded and reached inside his coat pocket. He pulled out the stun gun. "Before we start, you should carry the stun gun."

"No," Brett was quick to reply. "I'll have too much on me as it is. A weapon is too much."

Looking at the duffel bag on Brett's shoulder, Foster knew he was right. "All right," he said. "I just think we should understand the importance of the moment."

"Don't worry, I'm sure we are all aware of the importance of the moment."

Chapter 21
Iceberg!

Gallagher's watch read 11:35 p.m. The *Titanic* approached the silent and deadly iceberg floating in the North Atlantic Ocean. A shiver ran down Gallagher's back, but he was optimistic their plan would work. The possibility of committing theft on the high seas, while not interfering with history, had inherent risks. Yet he remained confident, as there were two important aspects in their corner. The first was they believed they knew the location of the *Rubáiyát*. The other was they knew the detailed historical events that would take place in a few hours.

The ticking clock of those minutes might also be their biggest obstacle. In only a matter of a few hours, the grand ocean liner RMS *Titanic* would be lying on the floor of the Atlantic Ocean, two-and-a-half miles below the surface. Once the *Titanic* struck the iceberg, the race against time to safely board a lifeboat would begin.

"Less than five minutes," Gallagher shared.

"Brett, take the lead," Foster said.

Brett moved forward, walking through the first-class promenade toward the officers' promenade. With the duffel bag hanging on his shoulder, he passed unobtrusively by the few passengers who were looking toward the stars or enjoying the brisk fresh air. However, the cold North Atlantic air did not keep anyone outside for long. Faces changed as often as the waves that crashed against the bow of the ship.

Reaching the end of the first-class promenade, near the barrier to the officers' promenade, Brett checked his watch: 11:38. A couple, who were holding hands, were walking from midship toward the three travelers. Dressed in formal evening attire, the man gave a casual hello as he passed them. The man glanced at the duffel bag. Gallagher thought the man was about to ask about the bag, and, to distract him, he knelt and pretended to tie his shoe. The couple continued walking and entered the stairwell to go below deck.

Brett put the bag down to open it and pulled out the ring of lock-picking tools. "Any minute."

Gallagher nodded upward as he stood. "Look up there. You can see the crow's nest. As soon as he calls 'iceberg,' it will be time."

Bracing for the moment, Gallagher felt a chill run up his back. The countdown to disaster gave a rush of emotions, including fear, excitement, and the thrill of the adventure. As the adrenaline flowed through his body, he heard the crew member atop the crow's nest shout, "Iceberg!"

Immediately, bells began ringing. Gallagher, Brett, and Foster were all caught off balance as the *Titanic* made a hard turn, trying to avoid the inevitable. Although the turn felt sharp, the large ship was only able to move a few degrees to avoid a direct impact into the iceberg. Within moments of turning, a grinding noise screeched through the ship as the enormous engines pushed the ocean liner into the iceberg.

The frozen mountain floating in the ocean punctured a hole in the lower part of the starboard side. The iceberg grabbed the steel hull and tore open the ship like a knife going through butter. As the engines pushed the ship forward, the iceberg lacerated the belly of the ship. In the middle of the North Atlantic Ocean, the *Titanic* had arrived at her destiny.

On the deck below their feet, Foster, Brett, and Gallagher felt the vibration of the engines. The grinding noise from the ship's wound cried through the night air as the forces of motion tore open a fatal gash along its side. Gallagher was about to grab the railing to brace himself, but the violent shaking stopped and the grinding noise ended as the engines were shut down and the *Titanic* passed the iceberg.

Being on the port side of the ship, Gallagher could not see the iceberg, but he did notice the ship was still moving forward. Unlike modern ships, the *Titanic* would need well over a mile to come to a full stop after shutting the engines off. Although two of the three propellers had the ability to operate in reverse, the captain ordered stop rather than full astern, and the massive ship continued forward.

Foster looked over to Brett, who was already holding the strap of the duffel bag with one hand and the railing with his other. "Just a moment. Give the officers time to get to the bridge." Foster looked toward the bridge.

"It looks like the officers are there." Foster turned to Brett. "Now, Brett."

Without responding, Brett placed the duffel bag on his shoulder and darted past the barrier, onto the officers' promenade, and quickly to the hatch door. He opened the steel hatch and entered.

Their mission had now begun.

Chapter 22
On Guard

Gallagher watched Brett disappear into the hatch of the officers' quarters. Although the screeching sound from the incident was no longer piercing the night air, the lurching and loud noise had startled most passengers. Those awake began asking the crew for immediate answers. Those who were awoken from sleep opened their cabin doors, looking for an answer to the disruption. The main deck soon filled with several passengers. Gallagher, along with Foster, watched the groups walk onto the deck and instinctively cross their arms from the cold air. Many would go to the side of the ship and look overboard to the dark sea below.

"I don't feel any head pain," Gallagher said to Foster. "Do you?"

"No. We haven't interfered with the course of history. The *Titanic* hit the iceberg."

"That's good." Gallagher was immediately disappointed with his choice of words.

"Let's move around the deck but stay close to the officers' promenade."

Walking to the midship, Gallagher noticed a woman holding on to her two children by their hands. A steward rushed down the other side of the deck. Two older gentlemen with smoking jackets stopped him and asked, "What the devil is going on?"

The steward, who kept his feet moving forward, raised his hands. "All is fine, sirs, but I must insist that I go to my assigned area."

The gentlemen were about to ask further questions, but the steward scurried away. From the stairwell, two members of the crew emerged and stopped near the gentlemen. "Ladies and gentlemen," one crew member called to all those who would listen. "Please, could you return to your evening activities?"

"What, by George, is going on around here?"

"Please, sir," the crew member responded. "We have been asked to assist passengers back inside, as the temperature outside is very cold. I would be happy to escort you, sir." He pointed to the stairwell as another four officers walked hurriedly from the doorway. The officers did not stop and made their way across the first-class promenade, onto the officers' promenade, and into the hatch where Brett had entered moments ago.

Gallagher looked across the deck toward Foster as they both watched the officers enter the hatch. *I'm sure they're going to the bridge,* Gallagher thought.

Foster crossed the deck and stood next to Gallagher. He could see Gallagher was worried about Brett getting caught. "Brett had enough time to enter the first officer's cabin by the time those officers arrived. Plus, no headache. He's inside."

Changing his thoughts, Gallagher turned back to the stairwell as the two crew assisted the gentlemen down the stairs. Panic had not yet overcome the passengers, and the crew had appeared to remain calm. The ship did not feel like she was sinking, and no general alarm sounded, nor had abandon ship been called. The passengers who arrived on the deck to check on the mysterious circumstances were now returning inside. Gallagher was surprised how the *Titanic* seemed to sail normally following the accident with the iceberg.

Chapter 23
Murdoch's Cabin

Upon entering the officers' quarters passageway, Brett looked both ways for anyone who would see him. The passageway was empty, and he was alone. At the end of the corridor, he saw the door that led to the bridge and wheelhouse. He turned left and went to the fourth cabin door.

Brett was pleased to see on the door, below an inside porthole, a metallic plaque that read "F/O." He looked at the easily pickable lock on First Officer Murdoch's cabin, pulled out the ring of picks, and placed the correct lockpick into the bore. After a moment of jiggling the pin tumblers, the lock opened. Looking once more down the passageway for any witnesses, he saw he was still alone.

Opening the door, Brett slipped into the dark cabin and slowly closed the door behind him. Waiting a minute for any warnings, he took a deep breath and opened the bag. He could still hear and feel the engine vibrating as the *Titanic* steamed ahead, even though the short-lived battle against Mother Nature was lost.

Reaching into the unclasped duffel bag, Brett pulled out the small Japanese flashlight and turned it on. The flashlight illuminated the cabin from its modified D batteries. Scanning the cabin, he saw the curtains of the port window were closed. Brett knew outside the window was the promenade where Gallagher and Foster stood on guard.

Below the window, there was a small single bed. On the wall of the cabin was a desk and chair. At a glance, Brett knew the safe was not hidden in the side drawers of the desk. The hand-sized drawers were too small to hold a safe. Above the desk was a small wooden cupboard. There was also not enough room in the cupboard for a safe. Across from the desk, there were floor-to-ceiling cabinets. Brett moved to the cabinets and was about to open the two center doors when he heard the promenade hatch open and footsteps outside the cabin.

He immediately turned off the flashlight and listened. The footsteps scurried past the cabin, presumably heading to the bridge. Waiting a minute to ensure the passageway was again empty of crew, Brett turned the light back on and scanned the open cabinet. Inside, he saw neatly ironed clothes, white shirts hanging next to blue jackets with gold bands around the wrists.

At the bottom of the right side of the cabinet was a wooden door. Brett reached down and opened the door to expose a small safe. The safe was green and had a single combination dial centered on the door. The safe did not have a handle and was opened by pulling the combination dial after unlocking.

"Easy," he said aloud.

Without hesitating, Brett knelt and set the duffel bag down. He reached into the bag, removed the hand drill, and placed the drill next to his foot. Brett then placed the flashlight on top of the bag with the light pointing toward the safe. Placing his hand against the combination tumbler, he closed his eyes and turned the combination lock, deciding where his drill point would be. After a moment, Brett opened his eyes and looked at the tip of his index finger. He knew where he was going to drill.

Picking up the hand drill, he placed the tip of the diamond bit where he held his finger, just outside the axis of the combination tumbler. He manually turned the drill to score the steel and begin a groove into the safe's door. Once the groove was started, Brett unclasped and removed the spindle crank. He then picked up the flashlight, unscrewed the back, and placed the flashlight firmly onto the drill's terminals.

Pushing the flashlight's on switch, the modified D batteries turned the drill, and Brett placed the drill into the groove on the safe's door. Metal shavings fell from the safe door with a quiet sound. As he drilled, he thought he could feel the ship beginning to trim forward. Fighting off the distraction of the sinking ship, he leaned harder into the flashlight/drill to help cut faster into the steel safe. Sweat was building up on his brow as the suspense of the situation made his heart beat faster.

The diamond bit became hot as it drilled through the steel. Minutes passed, and the sweat was now running down Brett's forehead and along his cheek. He heard the hatch open again and more footsteps. He paused the drill and held his breath as the crew passed outside the cabin. The crew were speaking, and one said to the other that they needed to get to their assigned area immediately.

After the crew entered the bridge from the passageway, Brett glanced at his watch before restarting the drill—11:50. About ten minutes before Captain Smith called for the lifeboats to be readied for launch. He shook his brow to cause the sweat to fly away from his eyes. Below his feet, he felt the deck slowly pitch as the bow of the *Titanic* dipped into the Atlantic Ocean.

Brett resumed drilling, pushing his body weight into the hand drill. After another minute, the drill finally broke through the other side of the steel door and, hopefully, strained the key bolt of the safe. Reversing the bit, Brett removed the hand drill and blew the shavings away. Turning the flashlight onto the hole in the safe, he pulled on the tumbler. The door did not open. Leveraging his foot on the cabinet, Brett pulled vigorously on the safe door.

The door did not budge.

Chapter 24
Promenade Deck

Gallagher could feel the bow of the ship beginning to sink beneath the waves. Like a subtle descent on an airplane, he felt the deck below his feet incline and sink slowly into the ocean. Foster remained focused on being an outlook for prying eyes near the officers' quarters, particularly from the crew. He walked over to the middle of the promenade as passengers began to return to the boat deck. Foster looked past the passengers to watch the crew. The crew were calming the passengers and were not aware of anything other than the immediate emergency.

Foster looked at his watch and was now concerned about the amount of time Brett was taking. He walked back to Gallagher and leaned into his ear. "Brett has been in there too long. This shouldn't take him that long. It's coming up on midnight."

"We still have time," Gallagher replied. "They haven't even begun to prepare the lifeboats. Things still look calm."

"He shouldn't be taking this long." Foster looked toward the row of lifeboats and then instinctively paced back toward the officers' promenade, hoping to see Brett emerge from the hatchway.

Gallagher moved to the center of the deck and listened to the crew for anything suspicious. They were calm and poised, preoccupied with calming the passengers following the collision, oblivious to the high-crime theft of the *Rubáiyát* taking place only meters from where he was standing. Gallagher noticed a family with only the mother and three children standing on deck. He thought the family was the same from the tender. A crewmember was speaking to the mother, and Gallagher wondered if the abandon-ship order had been called and she was being told to prepare to enter a lifeboat. Momentarily lost in thought, Gallagher did not notice a man walk up from behind. "You there, man, do you need my help?"

Gallagher turned, startled by the question. After quickly gathering his composure, he shrugged his shoulders and remained silent. "I see. You are not crew." The man gave one nod and walked aft on the main deck.

As Gallagher watched the man walk around the corner, an officer approached from his other side. "You there. What are you doing?"

Turning around, Gallagher immediately recognized the navy-blue uniform of the White Star Line officer. The officer was a heavyset man, standing directly in front of them. Still feeling awkward, he again shrugged his shoulders.

"What does that mean?" The officer walked around him and looked to where the first man had walked off to. "Are you with Mr. Gracie?"

"Mr. Gracie?"

"Yes, you were just talking to Mr. Gracie. Are you with him?" Without waiting for a response, the officer added, "Look here, we are only asking for women and children on the deck."

"Why?" Gallagher was trying to compose himself. "Is the ship sinking?"

"See here, now," the officer stated. "We'll have none of that talk aboard this ship. You're not to be frightening the passengers. We do this for your safety to ensure our women and children are not placed in harm's way. Now then, what stateroom are you in?"

Gallagher paused.

"What deck, man? What deck is your stateroom?"

"F Deck."

"F Deck, you say?" the officer almost barked. "We are not calling F Deck at this time. You need to return to your stateroom."

Nervously, Gallagher remained still as Foster walked up, speaking in a British accent. "I tell you, old man, I think neither of us realized where we were standing. You see, there was a woman running down the passageway, bleeding from her forehead. Said she was looking for a medic."

"What?"

"Oh, it's true," Gallagher added. "She said the ship was sinking and we were all doomed."

The officer chuckled. "The *Titanic*—sink? Don't be ridiculous!"

"That's exactly what I told my friend here." Foster nodded toward Gallagher. "She said something about finding a medic or an officer. We came here to see if we could help her. At least reassure her that the ship would remain afloat."

"Of course it shall," the officer sternly agreed. "This woman, where is she now?"

"She skirted off toward the rear of the ship. On the other side I believe." Foster pointed to the other side of the deck and toward the stern. "She was nearly in hysterics."

"I hope she will not frighten the other passengers," the officer added.

"Oh, dear, she certainly concerned us."

"Then I must go search her out," the officer said. "What does she look like?"

"All I remember was her name and the blood on her forehead."

"And we heard her name," Gallagher added.

"What is it?"

"Uh ... Molly Brown."

"Really?" The officer straightened up. "You expect me to believe a hysterical woman was able to give you her first and last name? Come with me, let's have a look-see and you can point this woman out to me." He began walking and turned to see Foster and Gallagher were standing still. "What are you two waiting for?" The officer raised his arm and motioned for them to follow.

Foster and Gallagher hesitated as a young ensign ran out from the stairwell. When the ensign noticed the officer, he did not catch his breath before talking. "Sir, Officer Boxhall has asked me to fetch you, sir. It seems there's been a bit of damage below. He is waiting at F Deck forward for you, sir."

"F Deck, you say." The officer glared at Gallagher. "All right, man, calm yourself down. Let's go have a talk with Mr. Boxhall and check the damage." He turned to Foster and then back to Gallagher. He thought, *There's something wrong with these two. Their story about a hysterical woman appears convenient.* "You two, do you know what the problem is down on F-Deck?"

"Yes, water is rising above the bulkheads and filling the forward compartments ..." Gallagher stopped himself too late.

"How could you possibly know that?"

Gallagher now froze, fearing his words may have caused interference with time, and braced for the crippling head pain that preceded his end. He stood motionless, awaiting de-existence.

"All right, you two. Why don't you two come with me below and explain these details? Ensign," the officer barked, "assist me in escorting these two passengers along with us to F-Deck. Let's see how they know about this iceberg."

Gallagher turned to Foster, surprised that they did not de-exist. Foster read his eyes and nodded in agreement. The ensign came around behind Gallagher and Foster. The two followed the officer down the stairs toward F-Deck, where the iceberg had pierced the hull of the ship, and where the Atlantic Ocean was filling her bowels.

Chapter 25
Separated

Brett continued to struggle in futility. He was unable to open the safe door. Replacing the hand drill back into the hole, Brett again tried to loosen the lock by enlarging the boring. The initial hole may not have made the lock weak enough to bypass the locking mechanism. He pulled the drill out and pulled again. The door remained locked. Brett stood back, trying to best assess the situation. As he stared at the safe, he heard a loud creaking noise run up the bow of the ship.

"Not good," he said out loud. "Not good at all." The clock was racing, and time was running out faster than expected. Brett made the decision that he was going to use the C-4. He checked his pocket and found the lighting fuse, but Foster had the explosive. He needed to get to Foster on the Promenade Deck. Sliding the duffel bag under Murdoch's bed, he walked to the door, slowly opened it, and looked down the corridor toward the wheelhouse door.

He could hear voices from behind the door, but no one was in the passageway. Opening the cabin door further, he peeked in the other direction. Seeing both directions clear, he moved quickly to the hatch and exited onto the officers' promenade. Moving to a casual walk once outside on the boat deck, Brett clasped his hands behind his back. As he walked, he could feel the incline had become greater as the ship continued to take on water.

Nearing the first-class promenade, he saw many passengers who appeared to walk around aimlessly or were standing in small clusters. A few glanced at Brett in hope of answers as he passed the barrier from the officers' restricted promenade to the public deck area.

"Excuse me," a woman asked, "are you able to help?"

"I'm sorry, ma'am," Brett quickly replied. "I was just looking for someone to speak to as well. But I wasn't able to find anyone over there." He pointed to the officers' promenade. The woman sighed and turned and continued her search for someone who could help her.

Brett moved to the first-class entrance to meet Foster and Gallagher. But neither was there. He looked back on the promenade to see if his fellow travelers were on the deck. The crewmembers, who were scattered throughout, were busy providing comforting words to the women and children. There was a sense of calm as the passengers waited patiently, breathing the cold evening air of the North Atlantic. There were a few complaints, but mostly about being outside in the cold or fussy children who were awakened from their sleep.

Brett looked past the crowd to the sundeck chairs stacked against the bulkhead. He maneuvered himself through the horde of men, women, and children idly standing on the deck. Reaching the bulkhead, he bent down and looked into the alcove of stacked chairs. Concealed in between the chairs, Brett recognized the blankets hidden by Foster earlier. Foster and Gallagher could still be nearby. Brett walked back to the first-class entrance and again crossed the boat deck to the starboard side of the ship.

Exiting onto the starboard promenade, he breathed the cold outside air deeply as he looked at the passengers standing near Lifeboat 7. Foster and Gallagher were nowhere to be found. Brett shook his head in frustration and made his way back to the port side, moving quickly.

On the port promenade, Brett scanned the passengers, who were mostly women and children. He moved along the port side of the main boat deck, careful not to bump or knock over a child. He moved swiftly throughout the deck, searching for his two friends. There was still no sign of Foster or Gallagher. Brett was becoming increasingly concerned. The plans to obtain the *Rubáiyát* and escape the ship to safety would fail if he did find Foster and get the C-4 to blow open the safe.

"Not good," Brett whispered under his breath.

Chapter 26
Abandon Ship

As midnight passed, Captain Smith had not yet ordered the lifeboats to be launched. Although emergency protocols had crewmembers preparing women and children on the boat deck, Smith held off on ordering the abandon-ship signal. Yet the captain knew the call was only a matter of minutes, or possibly seconds, away as the flood of water continued filling the forward compartments. He was told the ship would founder and inevitably sink.

The ship's fate, although known to those on the bridge, was still unknown to the officer who led Foster and Gallagher down five decks of stairs. Walking down the stairs was not difficult, but Gallagher knew the return to the main deck was going to be winding. Elevator lifts were still a rare luxury in 1912, and the crew of the *Titanic* had not been spoiled with the gift of a mechanical box to move them up and down the ship.

As the officer neared F-Deck, Gallagher noticed the passageway was clear of passengers. He also noted that the officer was panting and beginning to sweat. The officer gulped air and called to the ensign, who still stood behind Foster and Gallagher. "Where is Mr. Boxhall, Ensign?"

The ensign pointed to a hatch. "Just ahead, sir. When I came to find you, Mr. Boxhall was outside the companionway to Boiler Room 6."

Just then, Boxhall opened the watertight door that led to the companionway. Seeing the officer, Boxhall rushed to his side, unaware two passengers were standing nearby. Boxhall whispered to the officer's ear, "We have a dire concern, sir. Water is filling up Boiler Room 6 rather quickly."

Forgetting his train of thought regarding the two passengers, the officer moved with Boxhall through the companionway. "Hurry up, man. Show me."

The ensign, who remained with Foster and Gallagher, watched Boxhall and the officer descend into the boiler room, leaving the hatch door slightly ajar. From the corner of his eyes, he saw Gallagher and Foster begin to move and put his arm out. "You'll need to wait just a bit more."

Both stopped and looked toward the ajar companionway. Gallagher peered through the opening and could see the platform and ladder that led to the boiler room. He could also see the shine of ocean water. The smell of the salt water fumed from the boiler room and sent a shiver down Gallagher's back. At the bottom of the platform ladder, crewmembers, engineers, and ship's firemen were wading through the knee-deep water.

Gallagher then spotted the heavyset officer. Boxhall was no longer at his side, but rather a much smaller man. The little man had his hands raised in midair and was yelling at the officer.

"They know," Gallagher said.

Wide-eyed at their situation, Foster whispered in his ear, "We need to get out of here."

"I know," Gallagher responded with equal fear.

"Follow me." Foster began walking toward the stairs, followed by Gallagher.

The ensign moved to block the passageway, raising both arms. "I'm afraid you can't leave just yet."

"Oh, yes we can." Foster turned back toward the boiler room and began walking past the ensign.

As the ensign reached out to physically grab Gallagher, he saw Foster turn around and pull a weapon from his jacket. Foster raised the stun gun and pushed the electrode onto the side of the ensign's ribs. Foster pulled the trigger, releasing the projectile and sending an electric shock through the ensign's body. The man crumpled to the floor, resting on the steel bulkhead in the passageway of F-Deck.

Gallagher was surprised Foster took a risk of interfering with time. "Foster, what are you doing? Why risk de-existence?"

"We're out of time and need to leave *right now*." Foster stepped over the body and moved down the passageway toward the stairs. Gallagher felt his temples for a headache but no pain. He looked at the ensign, who appeared to be unconscious.

"Come on," Foster called. Gallagher stepped over the fallen ensign and followed.

Reaching the stairs, the two used the handrail to scale the steps as fast as possible. As they neared the main boat deck, the blaring noise of seven horns could be heard. Voices carried down the stairwell. "Abandon ship, abandon ship!"

Chapter 27
Seven Horns

Brett was standing too close to the emergency horn when all seven blasted. He grimaced in pain at the sound of the first horn. He walked away to minimize the blood-curdling noise of the remaining horns, but there was no place to go as the sound deafened the main deck. The seven horns signaled that Captain Smith had called for the *Titanic* to be abandoned. Dismayed at not being able to find Foster, Brett watched the crewmembers adjust from casually helping passengers to readying the lifeboats for launch. The lifeboats were being uncovered and positioned off the side of the ship before passengers were allowed to board.

Brett's heart was racing as his mind scrambled on how to get the *Rubáiyát* without the use of explosives. He could try drilling a second hole, but that would take too long for him to be able to reach an early lifeboat. He looked at his watch—12:15 a.m. Ten minutes were needed to prep the lifeboat and another ten to fifteen to board the craft. There was still time if he used a small explosive. If he could find Foster and get the C-4, he knew he could open the safe and secure the book.

He sprinted back to Lifeboat 7. As he neared the first-class entrance, he immediately noticed the crowd of passengers had tripled in size. Brett's sprint turned into a weave as he snaked in and out of families, passengers, and crew. As he passed each person, he looked at every face and then glanced to the next in search of either Foster or Gallagher. Near starboard Lifeboat 7, Brett could see the crewmembers lining up the women and children in anticipation of boarding. He overheard one crewmember reassure a family that the lifeboats were just a precaution, and the state of emergency should not last very long.

"But it's very cold," he heard one woman say. "My child isn't dressed for being out in that lifeboat." Brett thought of the many passengers who would feel the stinging pain of freezing water. He hoped the child would board the lifeboat.

Yet neither Foster nor Gallagher was nearby. Brett moved again through the first-class entrance and returned to the port side. Standing in the middle of the port deck, Brett could see in both directions, hoping Foster would see him. After a moment, he scurried forward to the officers' promenade.

As families waited to board the first lifeboat, a line of passengers formed alongside the walls of the first-class promenade and the officers' promenade. The barriers that divided the two sections were now open, and passengers were standing near the officers' quarters hatch. He would no longer be concerned about his unauthorized entry to the first officer's cabin being noticed.

He looked at his watch again—12:25. Brett had maybe fifteen minutes to find Foster and obtain the C-4, open the safe, and board one of the lifeboats.

Chapter 28
Lifeboat 7

The stairwell Gallagher and Foster were climbing was tilting. Gallagher knew ocean water was rapidly filling the forward compartments of the *Titanic*. As each compartment filled, the ship's unfortunate design allowed incoming water to spill over the top and into the next compartment; when six of the sixteen compartments were filled, the bow of the ship would sink to the point where she could no longer remain afloat, and the vessel was doomed.

As Gallagher moved up the stairwell, he noticed passengers were not crowding the steps to reach the top deck, where the lifeboats were located. Rather, passengers casually walked both up and down the steps. He found it odd that most did not acknowledge the peril after the abandon-ship horns blasted throughout the ship. Passengers remained composed as crewmembers moved, remarkably steadily, into their assigned duties.

Foster and Gallagher reached the main boat deck and moved past the idling passengers. Crewmembers had lined up the women and children in preparation of boarding lifeboats. There were a few stewards who helped mothers by holding the hands of children. Some women looked to their husbands, who were standing nearby, nodding to their wives reassuringly. Gallagher noticed one man shaking his head at the stewards. The man took his wife and children and walked toward the stern of the boat, presumably returning to their cabin.

Foster scanned the deck, but there was no sign of Brett. He feared something had gone wrong inside the first officer's cabin. He looked at his watch—12:35 a.m. "Damn," he said. "We were below deck for too long."

Gallagher called to Foster, "The tops are off the lifeboats. They're going to launch Number 7 any minute."

An officer walked up to the stewards and gave the order. "Ladies and gentlemen, may I have your attention, please?" The officer was waving his hands above his head to get the attention of the passengers. "For precautionary reasons, we are going to launch a few lifeboats. Of course, our magnificent ship is in no danger. Yet we are required to follow White Star safety procedures. As you know, women and children will be first to board the lifeboat. A steward will help secure your life vest, assist you onto the lifeboat, and remain with you until the ship is declared safe. Captain Smith will certainly appreciate your cooperation during this uncomfortable situation."

The reassuring words encouraged only a few passengers to come forward with their children. Most, however, stood back, whispering complaints of the inconvenience in having to leave the ship.

Gallagher looked stern to bow. "I don't see Brett, do you?"

"No. He may be looking for a way onto the lifeboats," Foster replied, not sharing his fear. Time was tight, and Foster had to make a decision. "We better make our way to Lifeboat 7."

Gallagher knew the bow was submerging deeper. He foresaw the next ninety minutes as the *Titanic* sank into the ocean so deeply that it raised the stern out of the water. "Let's keep looking."

"We can't wait," Foster said. "We need to stay with the plan. As difficult as it is, we've been separated. You know we need to get off this ship. If we wait, the lifeboats will be too crowded. Not to mention we may also be wanted when the ensign awakes from the stun."

Accepting the inescapable truth of the situation, Gallagher nodded once. Nearby, the stewards began preparing Lifeboat 5 for launch as the final passengers boarded Lifeboat 7, which was ready to be lowered from the crane into the ocean. A family was boarding the lifeboat, and the steward held out his hand to stop the father from boarding.

"They're not letting men board," Gallagher said angrily. "No wonder the lifeboats were half empty!"

"Come on." Foster pulled a pair of sunglasses from his pocket. He put the sunglasses on and grabbed hold of Gallagher's upper arm. "I'll play blind ... you do the talking."

Leading Foster, Gallagher slowly walked up to Lifeboat 7, making as little eye contact with the passengers as possible. The main reason to avoid eye contact was to be low key as the two moved past the queue of passengers. The second was not to feel sorry for those who would shortly lose their lives.

Using a whispered British accent, Gallagher cleared his throat. "Pardon me, sir, but my companion is blind. I noticed the launch was not filled. May he and I board?"

"I'm not exactly sure what you are asking, sir, but women and children need to be first," the steward replied.

Foster could not resist speaking up. "Here, here. I lost my sight in the South African War, and I fear I may get lost without my servant at my side."

The steward called a nearby officer. "Excuse me, Mr. Murdoch, could I see you please?"

First Officer William Murdoch walked to the steward. "Gentlemen, I am afraid we are only boarding women and children at this time." Foster and Gallagher stared at the man who they believed was on the bridge. Yet, standing before them was the man whose safe they had boarded the ship to rob. Murdoch was lean and well kept, his enduring appearance displaying his confidence in his command.

"Sir, my friend here, he's blind," Gallagher began.

"Just a moment, sir," Murdoch interrupted. The first officer looked into the lifeboat. "Are you ready to launch?"

"Yes, sir," the steward responded.

Murdoch turned to the passengers on the deck in front of Lifeboat 7. The majority of passengers who stood by the lifeboat were the husbands, fathers, or grandfathers of those inside the lifeboat. "It does appear there is an available seat. You may board this launch. But, unfortunately, only you."

"Excuse me, sir," Foster said. "I only fear that I may lose my manservant if separated. He is very apt and would be helpful in rowing."

Murdoch stared at Foster. Although his eyes were hidden behind the sunglasses, there was something familiar. "Do you and I know each other?"

"I don't believe so," Foster replied.

"Sir," the steward interrupted, "should we lower the lifeboat?"

Murdoch looked again to empty seats about the lifeboat. Turning back to Foster, he gave an affirmation to allow Gallagher to board. "Your servant may board as well. But he must help with the rowing."

"Understood, sir."

Gallagher aided Foster aboard and sat him quietly in the rear of the lifeboat. Gallagher moved center, next to the officer, and placed his hands on the oar. The cranes mounted to the side of the main deck lifted the boat up and over the side of the *Titanic*. The launch was lowered by ropes past the many decks toward the icy waters of the Atlantic.

As the freshly oiled wheels of the launch eased the wooden lifeboat toward the ocean, the two dozen passengers seated aboard watched the steel structure of the *Titanic* go by over the next five minutes. As the launch passed A-Deck, Gallagher looked up to the boat deck and could see a few men leaning over the side. The men appeared to be laughing at the people aboard the lifeboat. Gallagher could hear one of the men yelling, "Cowards! Hey, hey … look out! Watch what you're doing!"

Gallagher saw the head of Brett lean over the railing above. Brett called down, "C-4!"

Foster also heard Brett. Continuing his act as a blind man, he withheld looking up or calling back from the lifeboat. Rather, he reached in his pocket and pulled out the C-4. He held his hand cupped and called to Gallagher, "Mr. Gally, he must be looking for my sulfur clay. Could you please assist?"

Gallagher understood the message, reached to the rear of the lifeboat, and took the wrapped piece of C-4 from Foster. Gallagher looked up to the railing of the main deck. "Catch!"

Half-standing with his arm at an upward angle, Gallagher threw the explosive clay upward toward Brett. Brett reached out to grab the material, but the throw was short. The C-4 glided up to the railing and then fell back down, past the lifeboat and into the ocean. Foster, who was wearing dark glasses, could barely see the explosive fall past. He quickly removed the second and last piece of C-4 and handed it to Gallagher.

The officer aboard the lifeboat tugged at Gallagher's jacket. "Sit down this minute, man!"

"Last chance," he whispered to himself.

With all his might, Gallagher threw the C-4 up and over the railing of the main deck. The explosive went over Brett's head and fell behind him. Gallagher watched as Brett's head disappeared from the railing.

"Sorry, sir," Gallagher responded to the officer. He sat back down and kept looking upward to see if Brett would reappear. He did not.

Chapter 29
Composite C-4

Brett stood in the middle of the port side boat deck, frustrated by the safe not opening and by not being able to find Foster. He paused to watch the crew readying the first lifeboats. Looking at his watch, he saw the time was 12:36. *One more look on the starboard side*, he thought.

Crossing through the first-class entrance again, Brett made his way to Lifeboat 7. Squeezing through the passengers, he saw the launch had begun. The lifeboat was over the side, and he saw the crew lowering the ropes from the winch on the crane to the boat. Two crew guided the lifeboat down from the dual crane system. Two men, who each held a cocktail in one hand and appeared to be inebriated, walked to the railing between the crew.

"Cowards!" the two men arrogantly shouted over the railing simultaneously. One of the arrogant men was laughing. "Cowards!"

A thought occurred to Brett. A man would probably not call women or children cowards. Pushing through the idling passengers to move to the railing, Brett caused one of the arrogant men to spill his drink. "Hey, hey … look out! Watch what you're doing!"

Brett ignored him and looked overboard toward the lifeboat. Fifteen feet below, he spotted Foster and Gallagher sitting in the middle of the lifeboat as the cranes continued lowering the boat.

Gallagher looked up from the lifeboat and spotted Brett. Brett called down, "C-4!"

Gallagher's first throw ended up in the ocean, but on the second the C-4 sailed over Brett's head and landed behind him. Brett turned away from the railing and began looking for the C-4 on the wooden deck.

Passengers and crew were walking around, and Brett hoped the C-4 would not be destroyed by trampling feet. He spotted the wrapped paper with the explosive lying on the deck near a companionway.

"Excuse me, pardon me, excuse me, please!" Brett pleaded as he hurriedly moved passengers aside to retrieve the C-4. Nearly sliding onto the deck, Brett reached down and grabbed the explosive.

Being low to the deck, Brett placed his hand on the wooden planks and felt the ship sliding into the ocean. He checked his watch—12:40. Time was winding down. Shoving the C-4 into his coat pocket, he pushed his way through the crowd and passed through the first-class entrance. Crossing the first-class promenade, he hurried toward the officers' quarters, unconcerned by the gawking passengers standing against the bulkhead.

When Brett reached the entrance to the officers' quarters, he looked back toward the first-class promenade. He noticed the band was setting up their musical instruments to play for the passengers. Brett grabbed the hatch's handle, opened the door and slipped inside. Without checking the passageway, he made his way to Murdoch's cabin. He could still hear voices at the end of the passageway behind the door that led to the wheelhouse. He knew that inside Captain Smith stood on the bridge, overwhelmed by the pressure of knowing his ship would soon be lost. He could not hear Smith give the order, but he knew the ship's wireless was sending the first-ever distress call of oceanic vessels in trouble: SOS.

The SS *Californian* received the SOS. Captain Stanley Lord was awoken and called to the bridge. Ignorant of the new Morse code distress signal, Captain Lord observed the *Titanic*'s distress flares burst in a shower of white balls but assumed they were celebratory fireworks. Tired from a long day, Lord ignored the flares and went back to bed as the

Titanic slowly sank only ten miles from his ship. Captain Lord spent the remainder of his life explaining why he allowed fifteen hundred souls aboard the *Titanic* to perish.

In the officers' quarters passageway, Brett grabbed the handle of Murdoch's cabin door. Looking both ways to confirm no one had followed him, he opened the still-unlocked door and entered. Gently closing the door behind him, he closed his eyes for a moment and took a deep breath. Time was running out.

The smell of the recently drilled metal of the safe still lingered in the air. Brett reached under the bed and slid out the duffel bag. Picking up the flashlight, he turned it back on and set the light on the safe. He then pulled out the life vest and waterproof bladder bag. Placing the bladder bag on Murdoch's desk, he opened the clasps of the waterproof pouch. He then grabbed the lanolin from the duffel bag and stuffed the bulky jar in his pocket.

Pulling the C-4 from his coat pocket, he unwrapped the moldable clay. Peeling off half of the explosive, he inserted the gray material into the drilled hole using the tip of his pinky finger. Brett pushed the C-4 as far into the hole as possible. Once lodged in the hole, he pulled a fuse from his pocket and pressed one end into the clay.

With time running out, Brett reached into his pocket and took out the lighter. His thumb spun the wheel to light it, then he touched the flame to the end of the fuse, and the black-powder core sparkled. Moving to the side of the cabinet, Brett held his ears in anticipation of the explosion.

The fuse reached the C-4, and the explosion burst the safe open with a force that slammed the steel door into Brett's right arm and ribs. The severe blow caused Brett to keel over in pain, knocking the air from his body faster than he could breathe it in. He grabbed his ribs with his left hand and felt the pain radiate into his lungs. Kneeling on the floor, he slowly took a shallow breath. The smoke-filled air caused him to give a small, painful cough.

Brett took another breath, this one a little deeper. He fought off the urge to cough again. For a moment, he stayed kneeling while he regained a normal breathing pattern. He moved his right arm at the elbow. The bone was not broken but felt severely sprained. *Stupid*, he thought, as he realized he stood too near the safe.

He glanced back at the safe door. It had swung open as far as the hinges would allow but was now slowly closing. Brett reached up with his left hand and stopped it. He could feel the heat on the safe from the explosion, but the pain from his bruised ribs was worse. Using the heavy door as leverage, he pulled himself to his feet and picked up the flashlight.

Reopening the door, Brett searched the safe's contents. Throwing other objects to the ground in a frenzy, he soon found a large, sealed metal case just under a meter square. Pulling the heavy case out, he placed it onto the desk. Brett needed to know whether the case held the book. With a boost from the adrenaline shooting through his body, Brett pulled his lock-picking tools from his pocket and pried open the case.

Inside the case rested a linen cloth tied together with leather straps. Untying the straps, he slowly opened the cloth to reveal the jeweled *Rubáiyát*.

The book was much larger than Brett imagined. Foolishly, he'd thought the book would be similar to the leather-bound editions he saw in Müller's library. The jeweled *Rubáiyát* was three times the size of a hardcover book, four inches thick, and tipped the scales at twenty pounds. For a moment, the sinking ship was as distant a memory as the shining stars in the sky. Brett was awestruck by the spectacular book.

He shined the flashlight onto the dark-green leather binding, which was covered with hundreds of jewels. The images of golden peacocks were etched into the leather, with topaz jewels in the feathers, turquoise crests, and ruby eyes. He raised the book to see the back was a ravenous snake wound over the leather culminating with emerald eyes and ivory teeth. The border of the book was an amethyst grapevine. The book was unquestionably one of the most beautiful pieces of literary artwork ever. Müller chose his gifts well.

Chapter 30
The Lonely Ocean

Gallagher hoped Brett would jump down the fifteen feet to the lifeboat. Yet, as the lifeboat neared the surface of the sea, the fifteen feet turned into over fifty feet, and jumping was no longer an option for Brett. Looking at his watch, he saw the time was 12:45 a.m. To survive, Brett would need to finagle his way past the crew onto another early lifeboat. Looking from the bow to the midsection of the main deck, Gallagher saw the faces peering over the side. He was unable to hear what they were saying. The steel winch cranes on the deck were near to completing the task of lowering the lifeboat to the ocean's surface.

Gallagher could hear the waves crashing. As he held on to the seat between his legs, the lifeboat splashed into the water, and the boat's oar sprang down onto his lap. A cold mist of ocean water sprayed across his face and the other survivors aboard the lifeboat. Now bouncing up and down in the ocean, he was lost in thought, and he did not hear the steward order him to begin rowing the lifeboat away from the *Titanic.*

"You there, man!" The officer was now pointing at Gallagher. He snapped out of his deep thought and refocused his eyes on the officers sitting next to him. "Grab the oar! We need to move away from the ship."

Gallagher lifted the oar from his lap and began rowing without hesitation. As the lifeboat moved away from the ocean liner, the officer called, "Stroke ... stroke ... stroke."

The cadence of his voice helped Gallagher to row. The rowing was not about speed but rather about the rhythm. Lifting the oar out of the water and then moving it forward into the ocean and pulling again. Splashes of water continually moistened his hands and face. Rising over the ocean waves, the lifeboat often felt as though it was merely going up and down and not gaining any distance from the *Titanic*.

"Stroke ... stroke ... we need to be further from the ship. Stroke ... stroke ... stroke."

The brisk air seemed much colder closer to the ocean. On the main deck, the air had been tolerable. But aboard the lifeboat, covered with mists of water, Gallagher shivered from the chills. He believed the only thing that kept his body from shutting down was the continual rowing.

After a while, the officer said to relax the rowing. Apparently, he felt they had rowed a safe distance from a sinking ship. As the cold Atlantic air shot a brisk tingle down Gallagher's back, he looked at his watch—1:05. He looked toward the now-distant ship. The lifeboat was too far away to tell if Brett was on deck or not. Gallagher knew the crew, who'd been hesitant about allowing a blind man aboard a lifeboat, would surely not let Brett board one of the later launches. He peered through the night at lights shining from the *Titanic*.

Gallagher thought the tilt in the ship seemed to be quite minuscule compared to the dozen depictions of the ship sinking. The ship, from stern to bow, was still visible above water. From all appearances, it appeared the evacuation of the passengers may have been premature.

Gallagher looked at Foster, who was also watching the *Titanic* intently. Gallagher hoped no one on the lifeboat noticed the apparent blind man staring at the sinking ship. Glancing at the other survivors, he noticed all eyes were looking at the ship. The officer, sitting next to Gallagher, held on to his oar and spoke comforting words to the women and children, but still watched intently at the hopeless liner sink slowly into the ocean.

Chapter 31
Escape

Inside Murdoch's cabin, Brett lost time as he oscillated between the pain from his ribs and fascination with the *Rubáiyát*. When the giant ship lurched, bellowing out a deafening creak, Brett glanced at his watch—1:15 a.m.

Brett rewrapped the *Rubáiyát* with the linen cloth and slid it into the waterproof pouch. It barely fit into the rubber bag. Brett sealed the clasps and placed the strap around his neck, resting the strap on his left shoulder to avoid the weight on his injured side.

He then got the life vest on, feeling a stinging pain as he shrugged it over his shoulders. The discomfort along with the weight of the book had his brow dripping sweat. Tossing the flashlight into the duffel bag, he picked up the bag with his left hand.

Opening the door to the cabin, he stepped into the passageway. Standing before him was a crewmember who looked at him concernedly. "Excuse me, sir, did you hear that noise?" Not recognizing Brett, the crewmember changed his stare. "Just a moment. What were you doing in there, if you don't mind me asking?"

Brett, standing with the duffel bag in one hand and a canvas bag around his other shoulder, smiled and responded, "I was looking for the exit to the deck. Could you tell me where that is?"

Looking over his shoulder, the crewmember asked, "Where are you coming from?"

"I just came from the wheelhouse. Captain Smith sent me to bring these bags to Mr. Murdoch. Then I tripped and must have fallen into the door. But the captain wanted me to hurry." He nodded toward the wheelhouse. "He said it was something serious."

"Um, yes, I see ... the hatch. Well, if you ..." The crewmember stopped midsentence. "Was Lieutenant Murdoch in his cabin?"

"No, he ..." Suddenly, Brett was overcome with a splitting migraine headache. His muscles tightened as the pain shot into his head and down through his body. Brett had interfered with the past and was about to de-exist.

"Sir, are you okay?" the crewmember asked. "Did you hit your head?"

"Um, when I tripped, I think my head hit the door," he said through clenched teeth.

A voice was heard down the passageway from the wheelhouse door. "Moody, quick, man, hurry up!" The voice helped ease Brett's headache. He shook off the sudden pain.

The crewmember reached over Brett's throbbing arm and shut Murdoch's door completely. "You may follow me, and I can bring you to the boat deck. Lieutenant Murdoch is on the port side. Unfortunately, I'll need to tend to the starboard lifeboats at that point, but I suggest you have your head checked."

"Of course. Yes, I'll follow you. I'll be okay." Brett shook his head to clear the dissipating headache.

As the crewmember hastily moved toward the exit, Brett followed him to the hatch. Looking back to the end of the passageway, Brett watched the door to the wheelhouse close. The crewmember opened the hatch, and the two exited the officers' quarters.

On the deck, the crewmember did not give a farewell but moved quickly toward the aft lifeboats. Brett went to the first-class entrance. The tilt of the ship was more pronounced, and he leaned to keep balance. Carrying the duffel bag, his pace was slowed as he reached the starboard side. He nudged his way to the railing and noticed the four forward lifeboats had been lowered. The lowering ropes were all that remained from the cranes. Looking out onto the ocean, he could barely see one lifeboat rowing away from the ship.

He placed his foot on a lower rung of the railing and then lifted the duffel bag onto his leg. Without concern about who was looking, he lifted the bag over the top of the railing and threw it overboard. He stepped off the railing and tapped the rubber bladder strapped around his neck.

Brett looked at his watch—1:25 a.m. It was time to escape the *Titanic* with the jeweled *Rubáiyát*.

Chapter 32
The Night to Remember

Aboard the lifeboat, Gallagher held on to the oar as the vessel bobbed up and down on the waves of the Atlantic Ocean. He turned his wristwatch to see the time—1:45 a.m.

Lifeboat 7 was safely away from the *Titanic* and now huddled in the ocean with the other starboard lifeboats nearby. Gallagher gasped at the situation. Foster was safe, sitting quietly on the back of the lifeboat, nonchalantly looking through his darkened sunglasses in the direction of the *Titanic*. But Brett's safety was unknown. Gallagher did not know if Brett was on the ship or a lifeboat. Or even de-existed while attempting to steal the *Rubáiyát*.

From the rear of the lifeboat, Gallagher heard women and children weeping as they watched the bow of the *Titanic* sinking into the ocean. The end was nearing, and the survivors now knew the ship would sink. One woman on the lifeboat noticed flickering lights aboard the ship. "Are the lights going out?"

"No, not at all," the officer replied, still believing there was hope. "Nothing to worry about."

The survivors aboard Lifeboat 7, along with those aboard the lifeboats that floated nearby, were silent as they watched the lights flicker. Gallagher knew the flickering would not last much longer. The water was reaching the generators and fluctuating the power. Once the boilers broke from their mounting due to the pitch of the ship, the lights would go out completely. Soon, the only light would be from the distant stars. Gallagher watched the outline of the ship, still afloat in the black, merciless ocean.

The aft of the *Titanic* still held her buoyancy. The sounds of the passengers aboard the sinking ship reverberated across the ocean. Their desperate cries sent chills down Gallagher's spine. He wished he could have done something to help. But the past was written, and there was nothing that could be done but listen to the weeping of both the survivors and victims of the *Titanic*.

Chapter 33
Lanolin

Gasping for air as his bruised ribs limited his sprint, Brett moved quickly down the main deck past the engineers' promenade into the second-class promenade to board an aft lifeboat. He was too late. All four lifeboats on the starboard side had been launched. Looking across past the second-class entrance, he could see the dangling cables which had launched those lifeboats into the sea. Stopping to catch his breath, he leaned over the railing and looked onto the stern deck below.

Time had run out to board a lifeboat. The upward pitch of the ship became greater as the ship's bow sank further into the water. The muscles around his abdomen were tightening up as he fought the incline of the sinking ship. Passengers were scrambling past him to move as far aft as possible. Panic was taking over as calls for mercy were unheard. Looking up to the third smokestack, he could see the lights were still on. Maybe there was still some hope.

Looking to the second-class entrance, Brett saw a ladder that led from the main boat deck to a smaller upper decking above the stairwell. He grabbed the rung of the ladder with his good arm and pulled himself up the steps. Reaching the landing, he stood below the cosmetically added fourth smokestack. The fourth smokestack served no use but was installed to complement the other three operational ones.

On the upper decking, Brett took deep breaths against the pain. He was alone on the top of the stairwell. Passengers on the boat deck continued to scramble toward the stern. He took off his life vest, slowly raising it over his head. He then lifted the canvas bag holding the rubber bladder containing the *Rubáiyát* from his shoulder and placed the bag gently onto the decking. Brett next took off his jacket and unbuttoned and removed his shirt, fighting the pain from his injured arm and ribs.

From his pants pocket, Brett pulled out the jar of lanolin. Unscrewing the jar, he scooped the golden gel with three fingers and began spreading the waxy substance on his chest, belly, and arms. He scooped more lanolin and reached around to his back as far as he could. He grimaced from the pain as he tried to cover his spine with the gel.

Nearing the bottom of the jar, he took his index finger and swirled as much lanolin as he could onto his fingers and began spreading the remaining waxy substance onto his face. With one last circle of his finger along the rim of the jar, he spread the little remaining gel onto his ears. There was no more lanolin for his legs.

As the ship continued to creak and dip further into the ocean, Brett knew the stern would soon lift the three enormous propellers into the air. Dropping the jar onto the deck, he put his shirt and jacket back on. He kicked off both his boots and replaced the waterproof bag onto his shoulder. Lastly, he lifted his life vest over his body and the bag. Brett pulled the top strap tightly onto his body.

Brett climbed down from the upper decking on the wrought iron steps of the ladder, feeling the corrugated steel under his socks. He went back to the starboard side of the second-class promenade, near a lifeboat crane. He was now fighting the tilt, and the bottom of his socks had become wet. The lack of a grip on the wooden deck almost caused him to fall. If he were to fall, he could slide forward past the first-class promenade and back into the officers' promenade, placing him close to the sinking bow.

Brett grabbed the railing between two cranes. Taking a painful deep breath, he climbed over the top and held tight to the outside of the railing.

He looked down to the ocean for a place to jump but saw only darkness. As he was building up his courage, he heard the voices of the surrounding people. The voices were much different than they had been earlier. Passengers were now crying, and some were screaming as their fate became clear. Words of support now became words of farewell. Brett turned from the railing and looked toward the frightened passengers. His heart dropped, knowing what was to happen. The tear-filled sounds were the last words of children, husbands, wives, parents, and other family members.

To fight off the urge to comfort the passengers and join them in a farewell hug, Brett mustered his courage and turned to the dark ocean. Closing his eyes and taking a deep breath, he leaped from the railing as far as possible and into the icy waters of the North Atlantic.

When he landed hard on the surface of the freezing ocean, the air nearly escaped from his lungs. The cork life vest almost slipped from his body as it resisted being submerged. The stinging ice-cold water raced over his body as he sank under the surface. Brett was still conscious, and he swam upward, rising rapidly with assistance from the life vest. Reaching the surface, he could feel his body contracting and slowing down from the cold water as he took short breaths.

He began swimming away from the *Titanic* and toward the distant lifeboats. Kicking his feet and alternating his arms to propel himself forward, he pushed with all his might. The weight of the *Rubáiyát* strapped around his neck was a burden. His clothes were weighing him down in the freezing water. The muscles in his feet and legs moved slower and slower as the swimming became desperate. He fought the agony.

Kicking furiously, he fought to stay afloat, but his legs were beginning to spasm. The windmill of his arms kept him moving closer to the lifeboats as he paddled further away from the *Titanic*, fighting the pain as the cold air and his battered ribs constricted his lungs. He fought to take deep breaths. The lanolin did help to keep his upper body and face warm for a short while, but the cold ocean would soon win the battle.

Brett could feel a dizziness take over as he began to lose consciousness. With his strength fading, he lifted his arms out of the water and into the air. With a last breath, Brett hoped those in the lifeboats would see him when his crackling voice called out, "Help!"

The last memory he had before slipping into unconsciousness was something brushing up beside his head.

Chapter 34
The Old Woman

Gallagher thought he heard a call for help. Bending his ear toward the open water, he heard a call, almost like a child's voice. "Ovah there."

"Foster," Gallagher called across the lifeboat. "Do you hear a child calling?"

"I was just thinking the same thing," Foster replied.

An older woman sitting in between Foster and Gallagher overheard their conversation. "There's someone out in the water." The woman pointed to a nearby lifeboat. "The other lifeboat ... they are calling the person in the water."

Gallagher and Foster listened closer. "He's over there, Mommy ... he's over there!" a child called from the other lifeboat.

Gallagher heard men speaking. "Grab the oar ... pull him by the shoulders." He looked in the direction of the voices but could not see any details in the dark night.

An Irish woman leaned next to Foster. "I tink dey went after some fool who jumped into the ocean. I tink I saw 'im jump, I did. I swear, some fool was carryin' his luggage 'round 'is neck and holdin' to the outside of the railin'. I sure as t'ought he'd be good as dead if he hit the water. Catch a cold to put him in dah grave."

"A man jumped into the water?" Gallagher asked.

"Sure did," she called over the lifeboat. "I's seen him walk ta da side of that railing. The devil didn't have his day, 'cause he musta jumped and swam out to here."

"Do you think the other lifeboat went to save him?" Gallagher asked Foster more than the woman.

159

"It sure looks dat way. But I don't know how in dis cold water he swam. Good ting dah little lad called, and dah other boat went to help. Anod'er minute and he'da been at the bottom of the ocean."

No response from Gallagher or Foster. They turned toward the other lifeboat. An apprehensive smile grew on Gallagher's face as he hoped the fool who jumped in the freezing ocean was Brett. The two struggled to maintain a low profile and keep from displaying excitement. But still no de-existence. Gallagher wondered if the rescue of a person floating in the ocean would become a *Titanic* myth.

Chapter 35
Lifeboat 3

Moments earlier, several survivors in the rear of Lifeboat 3 had heard his call for help. The survivors immediately told the officer and the crew member, who held the oars of the lifeboat.

"He's over there, Mommy … he's over there!" The little boy wanted to stand, but his mother held him down in the seat of the boat. The officer directed the lifeboat to move to the man in the water. He lifted the oar from the oarlock and leaned toward the man.

"You, man," the officer called to Brett. "Grab the oar."

The man in the water had trouble reaching for the oar. Thankfully, the life vest kept him afloat, otherwise he would have sunk. The officer used his oar to guide the man toward the lifeboat, although the wooden paddle hit the man in the head. "Pull him by the shoulders."

The crewmember moved to the side of the officer. The two reached into the water and grabbed the man under his arms. "My God," the officer said, "he's dead heavy."

"The bag, sir." He pointed to the waterproof bag around Brett's shoulders. "There's a bag under the vest … around his neck."

The officer went to lift the bag over his head, but Brett found the strength to fend off losing it. "Noooo," he pleaded, using his remaining energy to fight off the crew from taking the bag.

Two women came to the sides of the officer and crewmember. "We'll help, sirs."

The officer and crew member reached back under Brett's arms while the women lifted him by the wrist. The four leaned back, and Brett's soaking body, along with the bag around his neck, were lifted into the lifeboat.

As they laid him in the wooden hull of the boat, Brett was shivering from near-fatal hypothermia, in pain from the cold air and near-frozen muscles. A survivor wrapped a blanket around him. He tried to thank the survivor, but his lips could no longer move. Only a mumbling gargle came out. Brett shut his eyes.

As he slipped into unconsciousness, he heard a man's voice. "Lucky fool, he could have died. This water is freezing. He must have the strength of ten men to make it so far from the ship."

"Here," a woman's voice said, "he's covered in something. Some type of oil or grease or something. Hand me a blanket and I'll wipe it off his face."

Sounds of movement surrounded his mind. The voices were distant, but Brett soon realized he was having his life vest removed as someone or some people were wiping the lanolin off his face and body. A dry blanket was wrapped over his shivering form.

Brett felt a warm hand on his forehead. "He's starting to warm up," someone said.

"Hey, mate," the officer softly called, "we wiped something off your face. What was it?"

His thoughts became clearer as consciousness returned. "I'm not ... it's nothing ... it's nothing." Brett tried to shrug his shoulders but just stared into the stars of the night sky as he lay in the lifeboat.

"Just relax, mate. You're safe now."

"Sir," a crewmember said, "another lifeboat is calling. They called over to say that a medic is aboard."

The officer stood and called to the approaching lifeboat. "Pull along to our side."

As the two lifeboats met each other, the oars were brought into the boat, and two stewards aboard reached their hands out to bring the boats side by side. Brett, cramped on the floor of the boat, was still feeling dizzy but warming up with the dry jacket and blanket. He could feel the two boats shaking as the passengers locked the two vessels together. The rocking waves of the ocean brought discomfort as he lay on the hard sole of the lifeboat.

He was looking upward at the night sky, but a face shadowed the stars as the officer leaned over him. "Hold on, just sit tight, mate. Someone is coming over to help."

"Is someone hurt?" a voice called. "I could come over and have a look. I'm a medic."

Dizziness was once again taking over Brett's consciousness.

The lifeboats rocked more, maybe from the waves or maybe from the medic moving to the lifeboat. Someone leaned close and whispered into Brett's ear. "Hang in there, help is near. We'll be aboard the *Carpathia* in no time." The voice was so familiar. "Do you understand, Brett?"

Brett did his best to reply. "Yes," he said in a weak voice. Turning his head to see who was speaking to him, the cold sent a shock throughout his body. In his fight, he closed his eyes and fell unconscious again, but not without realizing who the voice belonged to.

Gallagher looked up from Brett and told the survivors of both lifeboats, including Foster, who was still on the other lifeboat, "He's unconscious but alive."

Foster did not respond but gave out a sigh of relief.

Gallagher looked down at Brett and noticed the canvas waterproof bag wrapped around his neck. He leaned over Brett to check his vitals. With his other hand, Gallagher felt the canvas bag. There was a large object inside that must have been the *Rubáiyát*. The survivors who pulled Brett into the lifeboat moved to each side of Gallagher. "Is there anything we can do to help?"

Gallagher turned to each. "He fell unconscious from the shock of the water. Let's get his wet socks off and cover his head and feet." It was too risky to bring attention to himself by taking the canvas bag from Brett.

"Look! Something's happening to the ship," a survivor called. "The lights are flickering again."

"Oh, no. Is she going down?"

The survivors aboard both lifeboats watched as the lights went on and off aboard the *Titanic*. The ship's bow was now underwater, and the ocean had crawled halfway up the main boat deck. The flickering lasted for several moments before the illumination no longer reflected off the ocean's surface. With the only light from the stars, all the survivors could see was a dark outline of the ship, almost unseen in the night.

The survivors aboard the lifeboats watched as a flare was shot from middeck into the sky and cast light aboard the sinking vessel. Foster slid his dark sunglasses down his nose and looked toward the ship. The *Titanic*'s wheelhouse had sunk into the ocean. The stern of the ship was lifting from the water. As the propellers rose out of the ocean, water splashed from the spinning blades.

The illumination from the flare soon fizzled out, and darkness again took over. The distant stars would be the only light to shine on the dying ship. In the darkness, the survivors aboard the lifeboats could hear the cries from the passengers still aboard.

Suddenly, a grinding noise erupted across the ocean's surface, the sound of the steel ship fighting the impending catastrophe. As the stern lifted into the night, all objects aboard hurtled forward—tables, chairs, dishes, pianos, and the large boilers crashed to the front of the ship, pushing her bow deeper into the ocean.

A final crash burst through the air as the ship was torn from the deck to the keel between the second and third funnel, breaking the ship in two. Yet the *Titanic* fought courageously as the forward hull, still attached to the keel, folded into the ocean and immediately filled with water, bringing the stern section back down onto the ocean. The weight of the bow was too great, however, and the hull snapped from the stern section. The stern remained momentarily upright, resting atop the surface of the water.

Stars provided the only light to see the outline of the ship. Aboard Lifeboat 3, a survivor called out, "Wait! It came back down! I think the ship is going to ride it out!"

Gallagher knew differently. The stern section would float upright for a few minutes, but as the water filled the rear section, the ship slowly turned around and finally sank in the opposite direction from the forward hull. The rear section sank into the depths with air sealed into the airtight compartments. As the pressure of the ocean's depths became greater, it overpowered the trapped air pressure and squeezed the rear section, imploding the stern of the *Titanic* before it reached the abyssal floor of the ocean.

The unsinkable *Titanic* had sunk.

By 2:30 a.m. on April 15, 1912, destiny arrived as the forward and aft sections of RMS *Titanic* would rest for eternity on the seafloor, two miles below the surface of the Atlantic Ocean. Fifteen hundred perished.

Their souls would haunt the ship in her loneliness for nearly seventy-five years before a submersible research vessel would find the once-lost luxury liner.

From their lifeboats, the seven hundred passengers who survived the sinking listened to the final cries for help from those passengers who floated near the wreckage. In the dark, cold early morning, the cries from the floating passengers died off as the frozen waters of the Atlantic Ocean took their lives. The survivors sat quietly awaiting rescue.

Gallagher closed his eyes, overcome with sadness.

Chapter 36
The *Carpathia*

Unlike the SS *Californian*, the captain of the RMS *Carpathia*, Arthur Rostron, would go down in history as the savior of 706 survivors from the RMS *Titanic*, sunk on her maiden voyage in April 1912 in the Grand Banks, Atlantic Ocean. Sixty miles from the last known position of the *Titanic*, Captain Rostron received her wireless distress call at 12:20 a.m. and sailed to provide aid and assistance.

After receiving the distress call, the *Carpathia* sailed at full speed to the site in three hours. Arriving at the site at 3:30 a.m., Captain Rostron saw the partial debris of the *Titanic* floating in the water. He immediately began the rescue of the survivors floating aboard the lifeboats.

When the lifeboats were secured alongside the *Carpathia*, ropes were used to lift the survivors aboard. The *Titanic*'s officers and crew remained in the lifeboats and assisted children with their mothers and the injured to be hoisted aboard first. Brett was still semiconscious when a rope was fastened under his arms. For a moment, the officer on the lifeboat tried to remove the waterproof bag, but Brett resisted. The rope was secured, and he kept the bag tight to his body.

Foster continued pretending to be blind as he was given assistance with the rope. Once he was hoisted onto the deck of the *Carpathia*, Foster moved away from the other survivors and hid in the shadows of the steel mount of the mast.

Gallagher and the *Titanic* crew remained aboard Lifeboat 3. "You're next," the officer said, coiling the rope around Gallagher. Gallagher was hoisted up along the side of the ship. The lights of the *Carpathia* skimmed across the surface of the water. As he looked out onto the ocean, he thought he could see the outline of a grayish peak floating atop of the water. *Could it be the iceberg?* he thought.

Once on deck, Gallagher was untied, and he thanked the *Carpathia* crew. For a moment, he stood nearby to help with the remaining *Titanic* crewmembers still aboard Lifeboat 3. Seeing he was more in the way than helpful, Gallagher walked away to look for Foster. Gallagher found him middeck, sitting against a steel-riveted wall. Moving next to him, Gallagher sat. The two did not speak and quietly watched the *Carpathia* crew aid the *Titanic* survivors.

Chapter 37
The Infirmary

En route to New York City, the *Carpathia* was overcrowded with survivors from the *Titanic*. The survivors doubled the number of passengers on the ship, causing the majority of survivors to remain outside on the deck, while the elderly or infants were given cabin space. A makeshift infirmary was created in the ship's dining facility to attend to those who required medical care.

After being hoisted aboard, Brett was brought to the infirmary. Against his will, the canvas bag around his shoulders was removed and placed next to him as medical attention was provided. His feet and legs were covered in warm clothes. His ribs were wrapped tightly in bandages. The arm that was injured by the safe's door bursting open was placed into a sling, and he was draped with a warm blanket.

As the sun rose, Brett was feeling better and had come back to full awareness. He looked up to the steel ceiling of the makeshift hospital. Still resting his head, he turned to see the blank stares of the survivors who filled the room. A few still wept, but most just gazed into emptiness.

Brett reached under the blanket for the canvas bag that held the *Rubáiyát*. But the waterproof bag was not by his side. He turned his head the other direction, and sitting on a table next to him was the canvas bag. He reached over and slid the bag a few inches toward himself. Although he did not yet have the strength to lift the heavy *Rubáiyát*, he was able to feel that the book was still inside.

He sighed in relief. Keeping his hand on the bag, Brett closed his eyes.

"You're very lucky," a woman's voice said.

Momentarily startled, Brett opened his eyes and saw a woman wearing an evening gown. "You were in the water and nearly froze. They lifted you into a lifeboat and kept you as warm as possible. Then they brought you here."

"Where is here?"

"We're aboard another ship," she said. "I don't know the name, but you're in the dining ... rather, infirmary." The woman must have been aboard the *Titanic* and still wearing her evening clothes when she boarded the lifeboat. She looked at him with an unnerving strength. "Are you able to wiggle your toes?"

Brett closed his eyes and moved his toes. "Yes."

"Can you sit up?" The woman looked tired. Her eyes were puffy, and she looked exhausted.

Brett felt his cracked ribs. "Yes, but it hurts a bit."

"You can lie there." She walked and stood above his head. "Can you raise just your left arm?"

Brett took his hand off the canvas bag and slowly lifted his arm. Although painful, he felt the woman's warm touch as he raised his hand over his head.

"Good," she replied, looking down into his eyes. "You likely have very bruised ribs, but they don't appear to be broken. You're going to be okay. It may take a few days before they don't hurt. But you should have your strength back soon. Don't do anything in haste."

"I won't," he replied. As the woman turned to walk away, Brett called to her. "Were you on the *Titanic*?"

She did not turn around. "Yes."

Neither spoke as she walked away.

Brett reached back and held his hand on the canvas bag. He sighed and closed his eyes.

Chapter 38
Reunion

While Brett rested in the infirmary, Gallagher and Foster watched the sunrise in a quiet area near a dorade vent on the *Carpathia*'s boat deck. Crewmembers had passed out supplies for survivors, and they each secured a warm blanket and a sandwich. Before morning arrived, Foster was able to doze off for a few hours as he curled under the blanket. Gallagher, however, remained awake and looked in amazement at the splendor of the rescue ship.

The *Carpathia* exemplified the Industrial Revolution. The ship was nearly ten years older and less than half the size of the *Titanic* yet still held the glory of an early twentieth-century transatlantic ocean liner. Being a small liner, the *Carpathia* had only one smokestack but was rigged with four nineteenth-century sail masts that distinguished the ship. Gallagher tried to imagine what the liner would like with the sails raised. However, he knew from the rumble underneath the deck that steam engines were propelling the ship forward.

As the morning brought the warmth of the sun, Gallagher watched a small group of survivors walk onto the deck. A *Carpathia* steward was escorting the survivors and assisting them in finding their family or friends. Gallagher noticed they were wearing bandages. He tapped Foster on the arm. "Foster, look. Those are new bandages. They were treated and released from the infirmary. Now may be a good time to find Brett."

Foster nodded in agreement. He stood and walked over to a uniformed steward, who was assisting the survivors. Assuming a courteous and firm British accent, Foster interrupted the steward. "Pardon me, sir."

"Yes, sir," he replied. "May I help you?"

"It looks as though you came from the infirmary. Where is that located?"

"Well, sir, normally we have a small infirmary on Deck Two. However, with the number of passengers seeking medical treatment, the captain has used the crew's dining area to house the sick."

"And where is that?"

"Deck Four, sir." The steward pointed down. "The crew eats on the bottom of the ship."

"Thank you."

Foster and Gallagher found the nearest stairwell and made their way down to Deck Four. Reaching the former dining facility, the two found nearly fifty survivors lying on top of or sitting on the dining tables. The room was crowded with first-aid workers moving around to each table. Some of the workers were dressed in evening clothes, presumably having worn the clothes the night prior either on the *Titanic* or the *Carpathia*. Looking at the survivors, many were motionless with blank stares on their faces.

Keeping their heads down, Foster and Gallagher only glanced briefly at each patient as they passed. Their uninterested looks brought little attention as they searched for Brett. Workers were busy tending to the survivors. The tragedy of the disaster was apparent in the eyes of those quietly looking nowhere. The survivors stared into emptiness, in shock from a night they would never forget.

Circling the dining facility twice, Foster and Gallagher were unable to find Brett. "I didn't see him," Gallagher said, in an almost desperate tone.

"Me either," Foster replied. "Let's ask." He walked up to a woman who was tending to a little girl. "Pardon me, we're looking for a friend of ours."

The woman paused from her work and looked up. "What's their name?"

"Uh ... to tell you the truth, I don't know. He was a friend that I, or rather we, met on the ship before, uh ... well, he jumped into the water, and I was wondering if he was okay?"

"What does he look like?"

"Let's see ... he's somewhat—" Foster was interrupted.

"Is there a problem?"

Foster and Gallagher turned to see Brett holding the canvas bag around his neck with one arm and the other in a sling. Both Foster and Brett could not hold back their smiles of cheerfulness.

"Sorry, I was using the ... um, water closet." Brett then thanked the woman, who did not respond as she returned tending to the little girl. Looking around the makeshift hospital to see if anyone was listening, he continued, "I don't think anyone would mind if we leave and take a walk."

The three walked out of the makeshift hospital, passing a few weeping survivors standing at the exit. Brett led Foster and Gallagher out of the area and found a quiet, somewhat dark corner. He looked back down the passageway, still feeling as though he may have been followed.

Comfortable that they were alone, Gallagher finally said, "Well, did you get it?"

Brett smiled and slowly lifted the canvas bag from around his neck. Placing the bag gently onto the deck, he opened the clasps of the waterproof bag. "I got it. I got the *Rubáiyát*."

Brett gently slid the book out of the bag. The linen-wrapped book was still dry within the waterproof bladder of the canvas bag. Kneeling, he unwrapped the linen cloth and revealed the jeweled *Rubáiyát*. Even in the darkness, Foster and Gallagher could see the ornate jewels and golden design decorating the book.

"Oh, wow!" Gallagher exclaimed.

"Well done, Brett," Foster added.

Brett rewrapped the book, slid it back into the rubber bladder, and sealed the canvas bag. "A few times I thought they had taken the bag. But I held on to it and hoped my clutching hands would hold tight when I lost consciousness."

"We're sorry we weren't there to meet you," Foster began. "We had a situation where an officer took us below deck, and by the time we got away, the time ran out."

"I had my own situation," Brett replied.

Gallagher looked at the sling on Brett's arm. "What happened?"

"The safe didn't open, so I used the C-4 to blow the door. The explosion burst the safe door into my ribs and arm." Brett checked the seal of the bag and slowly placed the strap over his head and onto his shoulder. "My ribs are bruised pretty badly, and my arm is killing me. But they wrapped me up, so I'll be okay."

"That's good, Brett. I'm glad you're feeling better." Foster looked down the passageway toward stairs that led up to the deck. "We're back on the right track. For this part of the mission, let's keep a low profile and avoid people, including the press and whoever else will be there when we dock in New York." Foster looked down the passageway again. "Let's move up top."

Walking up the steps and out onto the boat deck, Brett immediately felt the glow of the sun on his face. "I feel like I haven't seen the sun for quite a while."

Foster was still thinking of their arrival in New York. "Be discreet and talk to no one unless you have to. By now, the word has reached New York about the *Titanic* catastrophe. So, let's assume every reporter in New York will want to interview survivors."

"After we get off the *Carpathia*, remember we still have to book passage back to Ireland," Gallagher added.

"When we arrive, we want to get off discreetly. Once we're away from the port, we may have to stay in the city for a few days until the next ship departs." Foster gave a reassuring smile. "The hard part is over."

Chapter 39
The *Errant*

Pier 54 at the Chelsea Piers in New York City was an asylum of news reporters, onlookers, and family members hoping to find their loved ones from aboard the *Titanic*. The news of the catastrophe had reached nearly everyone in New York by midafternoon following the sinking. The crowd eagerly waited for the rescue ship to reach port.

One the evening of April 18, 1912, three days after the tragic sinking, RMS *Carpathia* arrived at Pier 54. Upon docking, there were tears of happiness for the survivors as much as there were tears of sadness for those who perished. While the survivors disembarked down the gangplank toward the reception lounge, some stopped after clearing the gangplank and kissed the ground; others cried; but most walked off the ship in silence. Unbeknownst to the crowd, the three time travelers kept their heads down as they quietly slipped off the gangplank and made their way toward the pier's cargo storage. They weaved between the storage crates to avoid the customs and immigration officers.

Moving through the storage area, Foster, Gallagher, and Brett soon found the merchant gate to the port. The three walked past the guard at the gate without saying a word. Once outside Pier 54 in New York City, they walked down Fourteenth Street and found a hotel off the corner of Eighth and Fourteenth. The hotel was small and secluded but near enough to the pier for when it was time to return to Ireland.

The *Titanic* would serve one last purpose for the three travelers. Several last-minute cancellations allowed for easy booking on a small passenger ship recommended by Maurice. The SS *Errant*, which was even smaller than the *Carpathia*, sailed from New York City to Queenstown, Ireland. Passage was secured, and the ship would depart in two days.

After two days of waiting, Foster led the travelers aboard the *Errant* for their return to Ireland. Foster found their cabin easily, and the three remained there for most of the trip across the Atlantic Ocean. The voyage felt longer for the three men cramped inside their small cabin. Midway across the Atlantic, Brett's injured arm felt better, and he was able to remove the sling. However, he kept the canvas bag strapped around his shoulder for the duration. The only exception was when he used the washroom. At those times, Brett slipped the bag over and handed it to Foster. Returning to the cabin, Brett would take the canvas bag back.

Upon arriving in Ireland, the three disembarked from the *Errant* at the same port they had departed from on the *Titanic* almost two weeks earlier. The travelers secured horse-carriage transportation to the outskirts of Cork near a farmhouse. Any further, a driver could become suspicious, as riders were rarely dropped off in the middle of a field with practically nothing around.

As the three walked the remainder of the distance to the forty-seventh parallel, night was falling. Upon reaching the three shrubs to retrieve the satchel containing the 1937 clothes, Foster made the decision for the group to take a few minutes to rest before their journey to Germany. Before changing into the clean outfits, the three sat under the brisk night sky of southern Ireland.

Obtaining the jeweled *Rubáiyát* was only half of their mission. The travelers knew possible danger faced them when they returned to Nazi Berlin to finalize the trade for Wolfgang Müller's map. Gallagher was staring at the distant stars when, out of the corner of his eye, he caught

Foster standing. "It's time. Let's be on top of every step we take while in Germany. This is the other difficult part of our quest, and the people we'll be dealing with do not slap wrists."

Both Gallagher and Brett were quiet as they stood.

Foster pulled out the small return pad and opened the case. He moved around the grassy field until the light on the return pad became solid, identifying the location where the time cube would be generated. "Here," he said. "This is the place." Foster motioned for Gallagher and Brett to get closer, within the area where the cube would form and capture them to time travel to 1937.

Gallagher moved next to Foster. Brett tapped the canvas bag that held the *Rubáiyát* and then walked to Foster's other side. "Ready."

Once inside the portation area, Foster slid the switch on the pad to activate the preprogrammed command. The transmitted command bounced into the future, and the console inside the PTE truck read the information.

In the future, the colonel was pacing back and forth inside the PTE truck when the console received the signal. She watched the console begin to flash and generate the red laser lights. The colonel knew the time cube was being created in the past where the three travelers were continuing on the mission. She wondered if the *Titanic* trip had been successful.

In 1912 Ireland, Gallagher was watching the flowing branches of a distant yew tree. The time cube opened around the three, and the hazy gray cube enveloped their view. Their stomachs dropped as the sensation of time travel rushed through their bodies. The gray dissipated and, in the blink of an eye, the yew tree disappeared and was replaced by the brick alley in 1937 Berlin. The three stood in the alleyway down the street from Müller's home.

The time had arrived to trade the once-thought-lost jeweled copy of the *Rubáiyát* for the map of a hidden location in East Prussia that hopefully housed another lost treasure.

Chapter 40
The Deal

Twenty-five years of history had passed since the *Titanic* disaster. Yet Gallagher could see footprints in the dirt in the 1937 Berlin alley, footprints they had left as they departed the alley within the last hour to return to the future. Although time had passed for himself and his fellow travelers, Berlin had not changed. Gallagher pointed to the ground. "We're close to when we left. Look at our previous footprints. We've come and gone recently."

Brett tilted his head to better see the footprints. "How many minutes have passed since we left?"

Foster looked at the digital clock on the return pad. The time was 9:04 p.m. He shook his head, clearly upset. "It's already after nine o'clock. I hoped only fifteen minutes would have passed, but we're late for our agreed time to bring the book to Müller. We need to hurry."

Foster turned and rushed down the alley toward the street. Gallagher and Brett quietly followed. At the corner of the alleyway and the street, Foster stopped and listened. The city was quiet, and the street was dark. Nightfall cast an eerie feeling over the metropolis of Berlin. Pausing to look into the street, Foster glanced back to Gallagher and Brett. "Let's go." He walked cautiously to Müller's house. Gallagher and Brett again quietly followed in a straight line, blending into the shadows of the buildings.

As Gallagher sneaked down the street, he felt uneasy with the silence in the city. In the distance, he heard a dog barking—otherwise, the city seemed dead. He always envisioned Nazi Germany, particularly Berlin, to be a chaotic scene of violence and hate. However, it appeared the

Nazi stronghold ordered a strict curfew, where citizens kept themselves quietly hidden in the safety of their homes.

Reaching the edge of Müller's property, the three remained as close as possible to the neighboring building. Foster motioned for Gallagher and Brett to stay put while he climbed over the garden fence. Looking around at each window, all the lights were out in his house, with the exception of a lamp in the library window. The light in Müller's library was dim, and the curtains in the window were still open.

Foster hid behind the bush in the garden and peered through the library window. He was unable to see anyone inside. Neither Müller nor his niece was to be seen. Becoming suspicious, Foster climbed back over to the street and motioned for his friends to follow.

Returning to the alleyway, Foster looked up and down the street for any signs of police or military. Something did not feel right. He moved deeper into the alley, reached into his pocket, and pulled out the stun gun. "Brett, I want you to stay back while Gallagher and I go make the trade."

"Why, what did you see in the house?" Brett looked toward the street. "Is something wrong?"

"I'm not sure. No one was in the library when I looked through the window," Foster said. "I hope the authorities weren't called since we're a few minutes late. I would like you to wait here and look for any signs of trouble."

"Would you prefer if Gallagher waits back and I go?" Brett said. "I'm banged up a little, but I'm still good enough to help if needed."

"No, I'd like you to watch our backs. If anything should go wrong, there is one electrode remaining in the stun gun." He handed Brett the weapon.

Brett took the stun gun and nodded his understanding.

"Hand me the *Rubáiyát*." Brett lifted the canvas bag from his shoulder and handed it to Foster, who slipped the strap of the bag around his shoulder. "Now, Gallagher, let's go make the deal."

Foster moved to the corner of the alley and peered again onto the deserted street. He motioned with his head, and he and Gallagher edged their way along the adjoining building toward Müller's house. Upon reaching Müller's garden, the two climbed over the short fence and hid behind the bush. Foster cautiously checked the library window. There was still no sign of anyone inside. Turning to Gallagher, he motioned for them to move to the front door.

Gallagher took a deep breath and followed Foster through the garden. Foster knocked lightly on the door, and Müller immediately opened it. He'd clearly been waiting for his guests. Müller was wide-eyed and as fresh, as they had left him only a half hour earlier.

"Yah, come in, quickly." Müller waved Foster and Gallagher into the house and shut the door behind them.

Peering from the shadows of the alley, Brett had watched his friends sneak down the street to Müller's house. Holding on to the stun gun, the hair on his back rose. He feared that Gallagher and Foster were being led into a trap.

Chapter 41
The Library

Entering the house, Müller led Foster and Gallagher from the foyer to the library. On the other side of the library, Müller's niece appeared from a hallway that led to the back of the house. She crossed the room to the windows, glancing at her uncle. Subtly, she placed her hand on the dark red curtains.

"You are late," Müller said in a low voice.

"We were a little delayed," Foster began.

"Be quiet," Müller whispered in a strong German accent. "Der patrols are valking der neighborhood." He motioned to his niece, who peered outside the window and then fully shut the red curtains.

Gallagher turned to Foster. Foster shook down Gallagher's stare. Müller noticed the communication between the Americans. For a moment, he studied the faces of the strangers bearing gifts before talking. "I was beginning to think you were not returning."

"Time doesn't always go the way you want it to," replied Foster.

Müller agreed only with a nod. "Do you have the jeweled *Rubáiyát*?"

"Do you have the map?" Foster returned.

"I will not play any games," Müller snapped. "You came here with an offer. Now, do you have the jeweled *Rubáiyát* or not?"

Foster lifted the canvas bag from his shoulder and placed it onto the library table. Glancing at Müller's niece, who remained standing by the window, Foster unhooked the straps of the sealed sack. Opening the waterproof bladder, he slid out the priceless artifact, still wrapped in cloth.

He lifted the wrapped book and held it tightly to his chest. Foster looked sternly toward Müller.

Rubbing his chin, Müller did not react to seeing the object. He waited a moment for a reaction from the two Americans but only received a cold stare. Exhaling from his nose, Müller finally spoke. "Let me see what is wrapped."

Foster hesitated briefly then placed the book on the nearby table. Delicately opening the linen cloth, Foster flipped the cloth to the sides. Müller, now wide-eyed and full of expression, leaned forward to get a better look. Lit by the dim light of the library lamp, Müller squinted as though blinded by the brilliance of the jewels. He peered onto the jeweled *Rubáiyát*, an object he never thought he would see.

The German was taking short breaths, gasping for air as tears filled his eyes. The gems of the priceless artifact were stunningly beautiful to him. Gallagher knew he was obsessed. From the corner of his eye, he could also see Müller's niece staring motionless at the book. Her stillness made him nervous.

Foster interrupted Müller's gaze. "Well?"

The word made Müller come out of his spell as he continued to study the *Rubáiyát*. "Ja. Eine moment," he growled. For several minutes, he studied the beauty of the cover but never touched or opened the book.

Müller pulled his loupe from his pocket and examined the finer areas of the cover. He finally nodded with a selfish grin. "I do not believe my eyes. This is the actual jeweled *Rubáiyát*. How did this come to Berlin? You must tell me."

"Those details are not important. The *Rubáiyát* for the East Prussia map to the hidden location. If you renege on your side of the bargain, my friend and I will leave with our possession, and you may keep yours."

With a change in personality, Müller became very agreeable. "Of course, I will not go back on our deal. There is no point. The map is only for posterity. Koch told me himself, he wanted me to make the map purely in the event that he was not wanted by the Third Reich. Yet we both know that Herr Koch is well beloved by the German High Command. You can have the map." Müller motioned to his niece.

As if in a finely rehearsed play, his niece crossed the library to a bookshelf. Sliding a series of books to the side, she opened a hidden panel, which revealed a safe. She began spinning the wheel but paused after a few spins. Seeming to take her time, the blonde woman apologized for incorrectly doing the combination. She once again spun the dials, gradually releasing the locking mechanism. Finally, she opened the safe and pulled out a bound roll of thick paper.

The German's apparent delay was making Gallagher nervous. He sensed she was delaying intentionally and looked over to Foster, who was also beginning to show signs of unease. As a trickle of sweat rolled down the inside of his shirt, Gallagher glanced at his watch out of force of habit. Too much time was passing, he thought.

Chapter 42
Something Wicked

Several minutes had passed since Foster and Gallagher left for Müller's house. Brett tried to relax as he watched the street from the corner of the alley. Looking toward Müller's, he found the tranquility of the quiet city to be calming, almost peaceful. He took a deep breath through his nose. The smell of the city was serene and not fierce. For the first time in several weeks, Brett began to feel at ease. He was about to lean against the wall when he shook his head in disgust at his own actions. *No*, he thought to himself. *Nazi Germany is not peaceful.*

Refocusing his attention back toward Müller's house, Brett was unable to see what was going on inside. To get a better view, he walked out of the alley and down the street, remaining in the shadows of the neighboring buildings. Approaching Müller's garden, he then noticed something was different. The dim light from the library was gone. He looked closer to the library windows. There was no light because the curtains had been closed tight.

He climbed over the fence and peered into the window. Unable to see past the curtains into the library, Brett looked back to the street. Surprisingly, he noticed something moving in the darkness down the street in the opposite direction from where he had come from. As he focused on it, he saw it was a figure of a man moving closer. Brett crouched into the garden bush to better cloak himself in the shadows. He peeked out from the bush and watched the man quietly moving toward Müller's house.

The mysterious person appeared to be trying to go unnoticed, hiding along the walls of the neighboring buildings, similar to how Brett and his friends cloaked themselves. Brett considered leaving the garden and confronting the man until he noticed additional shadowy figures appear behind the man. As the group of men approached the house, the moonlight reflected off the helmets of armed soldiers of the Third Reich.

Brett bit his lower lip. He held his breath, hoping to slither deeper into the shadows of the garden. The soldiers were positioning themselves across the street from Müller's house.

Damn, Brett thought, *it's a set-up!*

Chapter 43
The Map

Idly standing inside the cartographer's house, Gallagher was becoming noticeably restless with the apparent evasiveness. Unknown to Foster and Gallagher, Müller had contacted the authorities the moment they had previously left the house. When Eva finally opened the safe and removed the map, she remained in place, and Müller walked over to her, positioning himself out of Gallagher's reach. Müller now held what appeared to be the map to the secret location in East Prussia containing the lost Amber Room. Yet if either Gallagher or Foster approached in a threatening way, he'd cleverly placed himself to counter any attack. Glancing to Eva, Gallagher noticed she had moved from the safe to the fireplace and stood near the chimney poker.

"My map itself is a piece of work," Müller rambled on, holding the map with both hands. "It may lead you to whatever you are looking for. But if I give it to you, it could also be considered treason against the Drittes Reich."

"I only need a copy. But ..." Foster picked up the jeweled *Rubáiyát* and held the book close to his chest. "We would still need to see the original map to check for accuracy."

Müller paused for a moment. He squinted, and greed seemed to fill his eyes as he stared at the *Rubáiyát* clutched in Foster's arms.

"Uncle," Eva said, breaking his stare. Müller turned to his niece. "I wonder where their other friend went to."

"Yes," Müller responded, taking a further step away from Gallagher. "What did happen to your friend?"

"*Er ist weg*," Gallagher responded in German. "He's gone."

Müller looked at him. "Gone? Where could he have gone in such a short …?"

"We're wasting time," Gallagher retorted.

Müller remained composed. "But you had a friend. Where is he now?"

"Is it not important," Foster interrupted sharply. "I can see you are not prepared to accept our offer. We will be leaving, and I'm saddened that we cannot make a trade." Pointing to the Gutenberg Bible, Foster directed Gallagher. "Pick up the Gutenberg. Our departure will serve as a reminder of what was lost."

Gallagher took the Gutenberg and followed Foster to exit the house. Müller's mind raced as he schemed how to keep the two from leaving. The authorities would arrive soon. Müller needed to stall. He would have to trade the map for the *Rubáiyát* and hope the authorities arrived before the two left his home. "Yes, yes, wait. I accept your offer." Müller moved forward with his arms blocking the door. "You somehow knew my weakness. I have always been modest, and I have no desire to be a part of history. That is the Führer's calling, not mine. And also …"

"Let me see the map," Foster insisted, still eyeing the door.

Müller turned to Eva, who nodded in approval. Gallagher noticed that Eva's hand now rested on the poker. Passively, Müller handed the map over to Foster, who immediately passed the rolled-up document to Gallagher for review.

Without hesitation, Gallagher walked to the library table and put the Gutenberg on the far side of the table. He unrolled the sheet of paper under the light of the lamp. Studying the terrain of the map, he recognized similar cartographic symbols from the map he inspected in the PTEUC. There were two locations shown on the sheet. The smaller of the two was a map of East Prussia. Gallagher recognized the Volkhov River, which flows from Lake Ilmen in the southern part of East Prussia, north to the great European lake, Lake Ladoga. Southwest of Lake Ladoga was a smaller, circular lake at the base of a mountainous range. The second, larger location on the map detailed the inner area of the circular lake and mountainous range. The east side of the circular lake was a road or trail that traversed its shore and led to an area simply marked with a red triangle at the base of a mountain.

Müller noticed Gallagher had his finger on the map. "The red triangle is the entrance to the cave that you seek."

Foster responded, "How far does the cave go into the mountain?"

"I have not been there, and I do not have the interior map. I only know the location, which he now holds." Müller pointed at Gallagher.

Foster turned to Gallagher. "Well?"

Gallagher nodded. "Yes. I believe this is it."

"Of course, it is the map you seek," Müller retorted.

Foster walked next to Gallagher and placed the *Rubáiyát* on the table. "We have what we want, and you have what you want," he said, glancing toward Gallagher. "It's time we leave. Let's go."

"Wait." It was Eva again.

Foster turned. Standing next to the fireplace, Müller's niece was pointing a German Luger pistol at his chest. "You cannot leave," she simply said.

"*Herr* Müller," Foster snapped, looking in the eyes of the cartographer. "What is the meaning of this? We have a deal."

"Hands up!" Eva barked.

Foster was startled by the command and raised his hands. Eva pointed the gun at Gallagher, who rolled up the map and raised the sheet above his head.

"Many things in Germany are different from your United States," Müller said coldly, moving back behind Eva. "We could not afford to take any chances. After you left, we contacted the authorities, and they are now on their way."

"Put the map on the table," Eva ordered, waving the gun at Gallagher.

Gallagher slowly lowered the rolled-up map and placed it back on the small table next to the *Rubáiyát*.

Calmly, Foster asked, "Why did you involve the authorities?"

"To have you arrested," Eva answered.

"Arrest us?" Gallagher replied. "For what?"

"Conspiracy and espionage against the Reich," Eva replied in a cold, ruthless tone. "If you are lucky, they will shoot you on the spot."

"Let it be on the street," Müller added.

Gallagher broke into a cold sweat. A thought suddenly appeared in his mind. Neither he nor Foster had de-existed, nor was there any crippling headache. Curiosity raced through his mind, wondering how there was yet no interference with time.

Eva took a step toward him, pointing the gun downward. Both Eva and Müller were standing too far from him to lunge and use force. From the corner of his eye, he noticed the red window curtains and remembered Brett was outside. Within a moment's breath, Gallagher reached over and opened a curtain, revealing the window overseeing the garden.

Eva racked the slide of the Luger, chambering a bullet into the barrel. She pointed the weapon at Gallagher and was about to squeeze the trigger and fire.

"Wait!" Müller called. He ran over to the curtains and partially closed them. Turning to Eva, he spoke in German. "*Kein blut in meinem haus.*" Gallagher knew he said, "No blood in my house."

Foster brought the attention away from the gun pointed at Gallagher. "Listen, there is no reason for this … you have the Gutenberg, the map, and the *Rubáiyát.*"

Eva raised her voice and pointed the gun at Foster. "You will not speak …" Before she could complete her vicious thought, the window erupted into shards of broken glass. Eva ducked down to avoid the flying glass. She swung her arm around to point the gun, knocking over the table and sending the *Rubáiyát* and the map to the floor. The other three in the room dropped down to the floor, preparing for an onslaught.

"*Liebchen*, get down. Gunfire from outside!" Müller called.

"We're being shot at, Uncle?" Eva said, carefully shaking some glass off her shoulder. "This is not the plan. *Die Schutzstaffel muss auf das Signal warten.*"

While Eva spoke to her uncle, Gallagher grabbed Foster's arm. "She just said the SS is waiting for a signal."

Foster pointed to a large rock on top of the pile of broken glass. "I think that rock was thrown through the window to warn us, and I have a good guess who." A sudden gunshot from a rifle rang out from outside, echoing through the broken window. The sharp sound hung in the air for a moment.

"That was a gun firing!" Gallagher exclaimed.

"Not in my house!" Müller reached over the table and turned off a light. Foster could hear him scream. *"Nicht mein haus!"*

Foster glanced to his right and saw the table knocked over and the map and *Rubáiyát* laying on the floor. He took a deep breath as another round of gunfire rang outside the library window.

Chapter 44
Fire Escape

Darkness momentarily clouded Brett's eyes, and he felt as though he was going to lose consciousness. He was breathing heavily after running back to the alley. The running, combined with the loss of blood, was affecting his balance. The buildings on both sides of the dark alley were going out of focus. Hiding in the shadows of the alleyway, Brett leaned against a wall and felt his wound as the last few moments flashed through his mind.

The armed soldiers had arrived at Müller's house, and it was apparent to Brett that his friends had been led into a trap. The soldiers had set up around the perimeter of the house, ready for an ambush. Still hiding in the bush in Müller's garden, Brett assessed the situation as rapidly as possible. He guessed the troops had arrived on the next street over and moved in on foot. He quickly counted four soldiers. The first soldier was across the street from the house, while another appeared to be moving to flank the house from the opposite direction. The last two had remained down the street.

Once in position, the soldiers would soon reach his side of the house and begin positioning themselves near the garden. Before the soldiers had moved in on the house, Brett was pressed to make a choice. In a rushed decision to warn Foster and Gallagher, Brett had moved around the bush to the library window.

He'd been about to reach up and tap on the library window when the curtains opened. Brett crouched down low as the curtains again partially closed. Brett had lifted himself off the ground and peered into the window between the curtains. Inside, he'd seen Eva chambering a gun and pointing the weapon at Gallagher. Her eyes were filled with rage and she was about to shoot. Müller had approached the window, waving his hands in a downward motion, apparently asking his niece not to fire.

Brett had kneeled back down and reached around on the ground. He found a good-sized rock about six inches around. Picking the rock up to his shoulder, he'd momentarily grimaced from the pain squeezing his damaged ribs. Taking a breath, Brett flung the rock toward the library window.

Immediately upon the window shattering, the four soldiers had lost the element of surprise and raised their weapons. Realizing his error in bringing attention to himself, Brett had jumped out of the garden and begun running back to the dark alley. He'd heard the whizzing sound of gunfire. Nearing the corner of the alley, he'd felt a pinch in his arm as a bullet passed through his right bicep. The warm fluid of his blood flowed down his arm. Reaching the alley, he'd moved as fast as possible into the darkness.

From the alley, Brett could now hear the soldiers yelling. Their voices were still in the distance. *"Nein! Kehrt zu euren Positionen!"* The soldiers were ordered to return to positioning themselves surrounding Müller's house.

Brett felt the pain of the wound shoot through his body as though his arm was clamped in a vise. A painful pinching sensation stung his entire arm and shoulder. His heart was racing and pumping more blood out of his wound.

Looking closer, he could see the dark-red blood begin to soak his shirt sleeve. He was shot in the same arm that was previously hurt on the *Titanic*. The bullet had hit just below the shoulder. He fought off the lightheadedness and refocused his concentration. Brett squeezed his right fist and thought that was a good sign. The warm blood was now pouring down his sleeve and dripping off his hand like a leaking faucet. Although the pain was nerve wrenching, Brett thought it was tolerable.

Listening again to the sounds on the street, he faintly heard the soldiers. Brett was unsure what they were saying, but he could tell the soldiers were still in the distance, likely surrounding Müller's home, where he had thrown the rock. He breathed deeply to catch his breath. Slowly, he tore away a piece of his shirt from his injured arm. As he pulled, he grimaced from the involuntary movement of his wound. Although the torn piece was covered in blood, he wrapped the cloth around the wound. He teared up from the pain as he tied the bandage with his arm and used his teeth to tighten the tourniquet as much as possible.

Brett clamped his teeth down as his body pumped the necessary blood needed to keep up the energy. A blind courage drove him to save his friends or de-exist trying. Regaining his composure, Brett returned to the corner of the alley and peered down the street toward Müller's house. The four soldiers were in front of the house, and one was giving orders to the other three. Further down the street, he saw a dark truck arriving. Brett assumed the truck carried additional soldiers.

Brett dropped back into the shadows of the alley to consider his options. Regaining some strength, he cleared his head of the weariness still lingering in his eyes. Looking upward, he spotted a fire ladder for the three-story building. Brett thought he might be able to get to Müller's house from the roofs and help Foster and Gallagher escape.

Walking further into the alley, he found a metal garbage can to stand on to reach the fire-escape ladder. Lifting the garbage can with his good arm, he placed it under the fire escape. He stepped onto the lid and reached up to the base of the ladder. As he struggled to bring the ladder down from the rusty retractable levers, there was a squeaking grind as the steel springs deployed. "Damn," he whispered as the sound echoed in the alley.

He jumped down from the garbage can and darted further into the dark alley, bringing the ladder fully down. As the rusty ladder still squeaked, Brett ducked into a doorway alcove to hide. Looking toward the street, he waited to see if anyone appeared. The noise from the fire escape attracted one soldier, who appeared in silhouette from the streetlights.

Brett took a deep breath and backed as far into the alcove as possible. The soldier was looking down the alleyway, seeming to assess the source of the noise. After a few moments, he began walking down the alley toward Brett. The echoing footsteps of the soldier's boots grew louder as he neared.

The soldier stopped at the fire-escape ladder, which was slowly creaking upward as the springs retracted it back into its upright position. He could hear the soldier move the garbage can and then mumble, "*Was ist los?*"

Brett heard the soldier pull the ladder all the way down and then lift it up and bring it down again, listening to the creaking noise from the rusty springs. Peeking his head out of the alcove, Brett saw the soldier had finally left the alley, turning onto the street and presumably returning to Müller's house. Hopefully not to bring additional soldiers.

Brett took another deep breath and crept back to the fire escape. The soldier had left the ladder down. As Brett approached, the springs were again beginning to slowly lift the fire escape back to the upright position.

With little thought, Brett quietly climbed the ladder. Reaching the second-floor landing, he paused to see if he was followed. The alley was quiet, and Brett continued to the top of the ladder and used the mounting supports of the fire escape to lift himself onto the roof of the building. He moved to the rear of the building and looked for a way down to the neighboring roof. The next roof was ten feet below.

Looking to avoid an injury from a high jump, Brett noticed a small overhang, presumably over a door leading onto the lower roof. Brett lowered himself down to the overhang, and from there he dropped to the roof. He moved above the door support and lowered himself down to the top of the awning. From the awning, he lowered himself onto the roof. The next building was roughly the same height as the current building, and he stepped over the parapet from one roof to the other. He was now next to Müller's property.

Brett looked over the ledge into the dimly lit back yard. The yard was enclosed by a tall wooden fence that ran alongside the buildings next to the house. There was a door on the back of Müller's house. Opposite the home, there was a garage with a sloped roof. Lying down on his stomach, Brett slid his legs over the edge of the building and lowered himself onto the roof of the garage. He used the strength of his left arm to guide himself down the roof and into Müller's yard, dropping the last three feet. Grimacing in pain from the short fall, Brett stayed crouched down against the garage as he looked toward Müller's home. There were no lights on in the rear of the house.

Sliding along the garage, Brett reached the garage's rear pedestrian door. He turned the knob of the door and slowly eased it open. As he walked into the garage, light shined through the upper panes of glass of the two carriage doors. Brett was able to see a vehicle parked inside the garage. He knew the carriage doors opened on side hinges to allow the vehicle to exit and enter. Moving to the doors to unclasp the latch, he slowly opened one door to peek into the rear alleyway. A lamppost shined light down a single-lane alleyway that appeared to lead from Müller's garage to a side street. Crouching down, Brett opened the door further to look in the other directions. The alleyway ended at the building he had earlier scaled down.

Brett looked back into the dark garage, using the additional light from the lamppost to provide more detail. On the wall, next to the passenger door of the automobile, was a folding wooden ladder. Brett moved to the side of the vehicle and gently pulled the ladder down, fighting the burning sensation that was shooting through his arm. Grabbing the center rungs with both arms, he slowly walked the ladder out the carriage doors and into the alleyway. He unfolded the ladder and leaned it against the brick wall of the neighboring building. Although the ladder did not reach the top of the building, it was high enough to reach the roof and pull himself up.

Brett returned to the garage and closed the carriage doors but did not secure the door with the latch. He moved past the driver's side of the automobile and headed toward the rear of Müller's house.

Chapter 45
No Way Out

After the barrage of bullets had stopped, Eva was in a crouched combat position with her gun raised, looking between her uncle and the two Americans. Müller remained lying on the floor along with Foster and Gallagher. She waved the gun in a circular motion and pointed for the three to crawl out of the library and into the hallway. As Gallagher crawled, he reached over, took the map, and slipped it into his coat.

Once in the hallway, Eva slid her body up the wall and turned off the hallway light. As she returned low to the ground, Foster glared at her and said, "You shouldn't have called."

She sneered a twisted smile. "I am a loyal German, and I will not allow American scum to infiltrate our country."

Foster returned the smile. "Well, your fellow Germans are shooting at you."

"No. They are shooting at you."

No, they're shooting at Brett, Gallagher thought.

They heard more noise from outside as the soldiers positioned themselves around the house. Turning to Foster, Gallagher mumbled under his breath, "What are we going to do?"

"Quiet," Eva snapped.

Müller began speaking to Eva in German. "Liebchen, I need to get the jeweled Rubáiyát and my map. I think both fell to the floor when we were ambushed. Are you able to reach?"

Gallagher was able to translate what Müller told Eva. Eva stood up and looked toward the library. The table was knocked over, and Eva could see the large book, but there was no map.

"I only see the Rubáiyát," she called back to her uncle in German. "The map is not in there."

"Look, Herr Müller," Foster pleaded, "we probably don't have much time. Let's make—"

"I have told you not to speak!" Eva pointed the Luger at Foster. "Now you can die, American."

"No, Liebchen!"

Foster raised his hands and braced himself for the darkness.

Chapter 46
Diversion

Brett stood outside at the rear door of Müller's house, atop a wooden step. He reached for the doorknob and gently opened the door, listening for any creaking from the hinges. Hearing none, Brett slid into the rear of the house. He stood in a dark room, although some light reflecting off a white stove provided shadows of kitchen appliances. He turned to close the door as delicately as he'd opened it, but instead he left the door ajar.

Turning his ear to the front of the house, Brett listened. For a moment, there was no noise. Then he heard whispering. A woman's voice from the hallway. He tiptoed toward the hallway and listened to an angry voice. "I have told you not to speak! Now you can die, American."

"No, Liebchen!" Brett recognized the second voice as Müller's.

Using one eye to peer around the corner, Brett could see Eva pointing a gun at Foster. His two friends were curled up on the floor. Müller was kneeling in a pleading position and shaking his head. "Wait, wait, *bitte*. If my map is not in the library, then one of them must have it," he said to Eva.

Eva placed the gun's muzzle on Foster's forehead. "This time I shoot or you give me the map."

"I don't have the map!"

"Then I will remove your head from your shoulders."

"I don't have the map," Foster pleaded.

Brett saw Gallagher roll over to reveal his open jacket. "Don't do anything rash! I have the map. I'll give it back. I just have to stand up to pull it out of my coat."

Eva moved her gun from Foster and pointed it toward Gallagher. She waved the gun upward and Gallagher lifted himself to his feet. While he was opening his jacket to retrieve the map, the soldiers outside the house began yelling. "*Achtung! Verlassen Sie schnell das Haus!*" Gallagher dropped back onto the floor, not following the Germans' order to leave the house.

Müller called out to the soldiers from the hallway. "Wait ... *bitte warten!*"

The soldiers knew their suspects were hiding inside the home but Müller's apparent authority bought some time. Nevertheless, they were going to enter the house at any moment. Brett pulled away from the hallway and slipped back into the kitchen. He moved to the rear window, slid the curtains to the side, and looked for soldiers. The yard was quiet. The soldiers may have not been aware Müller's house had a back yard.

He could hear Müller call out to the soldiers. "*Wir verlassen das Haus! Zwei Minuten.*"

Brett understood, two minutes remained. He looked around the kitchen for some type of weapon, but the darkness made his search futile. He moved over to the stove to see if there was anything he could use. Moving his hands on top of the stove between the burners, he felt a box of matches.

There was time for one more distraction.

Sliding the matchbox open, Brett pulled three matches out and struck the tips to the side of the box. With the kitchen illuminated by the matches, he could now see the white stove more clearly.

Moving the lit matches over to the window, he held the flame to the bottom of the curtain until one side caught on fire. As the flame rose up the cloth, Brett dropped the matches and pulled the rod holding the flaming curtains off the window and turned toward the hallway.

Chapter 47
Fire

Remaining as close to the floor as possible, Foster and Gallagher lay still on the floor as Müller pleaded with the soldiers not to enter his home. "*Wir verlassen das Haus! Zwei Minuten.*"

Either desiring or fearing the loss of the *Rubáiyát*, Müller crawled along the floor like a tiger stalking its prey. Müller kept his head low to keep hidden from the soldiers on the street. Müller grabbed the jeweled book and rose into a crouch. Holding the book tightly and duck-walking, he returned to the hallway with the *Rubáiyát*. Once on the hallway carpet, Müller kneeled down and looked at Foster with envy in his eyes. "*Das is mine.*"

Foster spoke calmly to Müller. "There is no place for us to run, but we need—"

"Enough," Eva snapped and turned to Gallagher. "Stand up, American, and hand over the map!"

Gallagher slowly stood as he feared being shot either from a bullet from the soldiers outside or Eva inside. Rising to his feet, he held his hands out to show that he was not a threat. Eva waved her pistol, motioning Gallagher to open his coat and hand over the map. As he reached into his coat pocket, smoke filled his nostrils. Glancing past Eva, he saw a brightening glow as white smoke filled the hallway.

Müller was the second to smell the smoke and turned to see the kitchen curtains burning at the end of his hallway. Clutching the jeweled *Rubáiyát* with both arms, Müller showed no emotion. Gallagher noticed his calm reaction to the spreading fire and thought the response was somewhat frightening. Upon noticing the flames, Eva waved the gun at

Foster and Gallagher. Gallagher shrugged his shoulders while pulling his arm out of his jacket. "It wasn't me."

Müller shuffled toward the fire, keeping the precious *Rubáiyát* to his side, away from the growing flames. He was trying to stomp out the curtain, but the flames had now ignited the carpet runner that decorated the hallway.

Eva maintained her stoic assertiveness as her eyes alternated between the growing blaze and Foster and Gallagher. She could see that her uncle was unsuccessful in putting out the fire. Each time Müller stamped the burning curtains, another row of flames appeared on the carpet. The fire was now spreading and crawling up the wall. Pointing the Luger at Gallagher, Eva broke her steady aim when she called, "*Helfen*, Uncle?"

Like lightning, the response raced through Gallagher's mind. As the small fire turned into a catastrophic blaze before his eyes, Gallagher saw Eva's guard drop. Impulsively, he hurled himself toward her. Eva turned from the flames to see the charge and swung the gun toward Gallagher. As her arm straightened to fire the weapon, Gallagher grabbed her arm, and the weapon fired away from his body, striking the hallway wall inches from Foster's head.

Eva was strong for a woman, and the Luger still had bullets. As Gallagher fought her arm, she lifted her knee into his groin, sending pain through his body. With the moment of shock, she broke free, pushing Gallagher against the wall and pointed the Luger at his head. She foolishly added final words. "*Auf Wiedersehen*, American!"

Foster kneeled upward and lunged toward Eva, striking her like a defensive football player tackling a quarterback. Eva was rammed into the wall, knocking a nearby painting to the ground. Stunned, she sank to the floor, gasping for air.

While Foster kept her pinned to the wall, Gallagher, still feeling the pain in his groin, moved in on Eva and grabbed her bangs. He pulled her head forward and then pushed her skull against the wall as hard as he could. A bright white light filled Eva's eyes, knocking her unconscious.

The fire had spread from the curtains, up the wall, and now reached the ceiling. Not immediately noticing the scuffle with Eva, Müller had the *Rubáiyát* behind his back as he continued to stamp the floor with the sole of his shoe. Hearing the noise of the struggle, Müller turned to watch Foster tackle Eva and Gallagher knock her unconscious.

Turning his back to the flames, Müller brought the *Rubáiyát* in front of him and clasped the book with both hands. As he was about to advance on Foster, Brett appeared behind him from the kitchen, jumping over the burning carpet and grabbing Müller around his neck. Brett tightened his left arm, cutting off the blood supply from Müller's carotid arteries. Müller soon lost consciousness and dropped to the floor as the flames rose around Brett.

"Well done, Brett!" Gallagher cheered.

"No time," Brett uttered. "We need to go now." The flames were encircling the hallway. A drizzle of fire had dropped onto the fallen painting and was now smoldering. He prepared to jump back over the fire that led to the kitchen and guide Foster and Gallagher to the rear of the house.

"Wait," Foster said, pointing to the unconscious woman lying next to him. "Müller dies in the fire … but there was no mention of Eva. If we don't save her, this moment could lead to our de-existence. All of us."

"Maybe she just wasn't mentioned but still died," Gallagher said. "How do we know?"

Foster hesitated. There was no mention of a second death, only Müller's. Shaking his head, the conversation at the PTEUC flashed before his eyes. The colonel said the fire spread quickly, which he knew was true as the flames had now traveled to the ceiling above them. Once the fire reached the books in the library, the house would be incinerated.

Brett turned toward the fire that would soon block the exit to the kitchen. "Come on, we need to go. There's a way out. The kitchen goes to a back yard. We can go through the garage, which leads to an alley ..."

Foster looked down at Eva, who was still unconscious. The smoke would soon fill her lungs, and she would likely die of asphyxiation before burning to death. Looking up at Brett, he asked, "A back yard?"

"Yes," Brett said. "Let's move while we can still cross the flames!"

Foster kneeled and lifted Eva's small-framed, unconscious body over his shoulder. Before standing, Foster saw the reflection of the flames shining on the golden *Rubáiyát* sitting next to Müller's lifeless body. He held Eva on his shoulder with one arm and reached out and took the book with the other.

Gallagher felt the heat of the fire. "Give me the book."

"I've got it. Let's go." Standing up, Foster hurriedly crossed through the flames and ran to the kitchen. Behind him, Gallagher and Brett followed, both jumping over the flames on the ground, avoiding the fire climbing the wall.

In the kitchen, the light from the fire lit the back door. Foster placed the *Rubáiyát* on the counter and patted the flames on his pants with his free hand, still holding Eva on his shoulder. Brett passed him and opened the door, motioning toward the back yard. Foster picked up the *Rubáiyát* and carried the unconscious Eva past Brett and out of harm's way. Gallagher followed, and Brett closed the door behind him as the flames crawled into the kitchen.

"Over there," Brett whispered and pointed to the garage door.

Foster, who still had Eva on his shoulder while carrying the *Rubáiyát* in his other hand, led the way to the garage door. As he jogged to the door, Gallagher noticed Eva's arms swaying as she rested unconscious on Foster's shoulder. Brett hurried around Foster and opened the garage door. Gallagher came up the rear and looked back toward the house. Smoke was escaping from the upstairs windows as the flames reached the library. The fire would soon engulf the entire house. Gallagher entered the garage, and Brett shut the side door.

The small amount of light from the half-open garage door allowed Foster and Gallagher to see the parked vehicle. Foster placed Eva delicately on the concrete floor next to the car. Gallagher thought of the irony of saving the life of a person who had only minutes ago pointed a loaded pistol at both him and Foster. "I guess you were right," Gallagher added. "We're still here. If we had left her, it would have …" He did not complete the sentence.

Brett moved toward the half-open garage door and crouched down. "Come on. We need to do a little climbing." He ducked under the door. Foster and Gallagher followed.

Chapter 48
Rooftops

Foster and Gallagher crawled underneath the garage door and joined Brett in the alley, leaving the unconscious Eva lying on the garage floor. Brett was pointing up the ladder next to the neighboring building. "My arm is in bad shape and I'm not sure I can lift myself from the ladder to the roof. You go first and give me a hand."

Without a response, Gallagher immediately climbed up the ladder and lifted himself over the parapet onto the neighboring building's roof. From the greater height, Gallagher could see the plumes of smoke and hear the crackling of Müller's home burning. All those books in the library were being incinerated as the fire grew and combusted all in its path. Gallagher thought of the Gutenberg Bible that was left in the home and would soon be ravished by flames. As with many missions, some things were gained and some things were lost. Although the Gutenberg Bible was not an original, he still considered the loss of the book.

Foster called from the ladder, "Gallagher, take the *Rubáiyát*." At the top step of the ladder, he braced himself on the parapet wall and handed the *Rubáiyát* to Gallagher. Placing his hands on the edge on the parapet, he gave a kick off the top step of the ladder as he pulled himself over the edge and onto the roof. He then kneeled and placed his arms over the parapet. "Okay, Brett, come up slowly."

Gallagher set the *Rubáiyát* down and kneeled next to Foster. Brett climbed the ladder and lifted his left arm up for Gallagher and Foster to grab on to. Using their combined strength, Brett was hoisted up over the parapet and onto the roof.

Foster picked up the *Rubáiyát* as he stood. Gallagher helped Brett to his feet. "Where to now?"

"This way." Brett led the two over the rooftop, stepping over the parapet to the adjoining building. For the next building, Brett approached the door with the small overhang and pointed up the ten-foot wall. "Last hurdle. We need to climb up to the third floor of that building. There's a fire escape that leads down to the alley. We use the overhang to climb onto the roof."

"Gallagher, you go up first." Foster handed Brett the *Rubáiyát* and leaned his back on the wall to help Gallagher climb up onto the overhang. Once upon the overhang, Gallagher reached down and took the *Rubáiyát* and placed the book on the third-floor roof. He then helped Brett up, with Foster assisting from below. Once Brett was boosted onto the roof, Gallagher reached down and grabbed Foster's hand to assist him onto the overhang. The two then lifted themselves onto the higher roof.

Brett motioned toward the fire escape, which had now returned to the upright position. Reaching the mounts of the fire escape, Brett pointed down. "Down there is our alley."

Foster looked down the fire escape and saw there was a second-floor landing before reaching the alley. "Gallagher, go to the landing and spot Brett as he goes down. I'll assist him from above."

Gallagher lowered himself down and onto the ladder. His weight made the spring mechanism lower the metal stairs. The ladder folded downward, making the recognizable squeaking sound as the springs gave way under his weight. Climbing down the steps, Gallagher reached the landing and looked back up. He saw Brett and Foster motioning for him to return back up the ladder.

Unsure why, he looked down to the alley toward the street. Gallagher was startled by the silhouetted figure standing in the entrance to the alley. The soldier began to raise a rifle and focus the weapon toward Gallagher.

The shadowy figure called, "*Herunterkommen.*" The soldier wanted him to come down from the ladder. Gallagher could see the soldier was motioning his rifle in an upward fashion. From afar, it looked as though the soldier was lifting a whistle from a lanyard around his neck. If he was about to blow on a whistle to alert more soldiers, Gallagher had to do something immediately to stop the alarm from happening.

From the landing, he began pointing feverishly to the street. "*Unten auf der Straße. Hilfe! Schnell!*" Gallagher told the soldier he needed to go down the street immediately.

The figure took a step back and looked down the street toward Müller's house then walked back into the alley and held his whistle to his mouth. In the distance, the sound of fire engine bells could be heard.

Gallagher called again, telling the soldier the fire needed attention. "*Die flammen. Schnell!*"

The fire was engulfing Müller's home as expected. The soldier again moved backward and onto the street to look for the emergency vehicle, and he lowered his whistle. While the soldier was distracted, Gallagher stepped onto the bottom rung of the ladder. As the springs of the ladder creaked downward, Gallagher could see how close he was to the return location. If the soldier would leave, he and his friends were only seconds from escaping 1937.

Yet the soldier was again returning to the alley and looking up to the fire escape. Gallagher used the metal side rail supports to hide from him. Briefly looking down the alley, the man lifted his whistle again and began blowing. The fire engine bells grew louder, but Gallagher heard the whistle over the sounds of the fire truck. He could also hear stampeding heavy boots echoing off the walls in the alley as soldiers began converging from down the street.

Gallagher considered his options. Going up the fire escape would make him an easy target, as well as giving away the location of Foster and Brett. As the heavy boots stomping the bricked street grew louder, the soldier walked back out of the alley and called to the approaching support. During that moment, Gallagher used the metal railing to slide down the ladder to the bottom. At the bottom, he crouched down and moved alongside the building, hoping to hide in the shadows.

Gallagher heard the boots from the soldiers stopping at the entrance to the alley. In all likelihood, they'd heard him drop to the ground. Staying as close to the wall as possible, Gallagher sneaked further back into the alley until he found the doorway alcove where Brett had hidden earlier. Staying low, Gallagher entered the dark alcove and hugged the door to hide.

Peering from the alcove, he could see one of the soldiers shining a flashlight up at the fire escape. The soldier began to walk to the fire escape, using the flashlight to scan the dark alley while two other soldiers remained at the entrance to the alley with their rifles in ready position. Gallagher took a deep breath and pushed himself as far into the alcove as he could.

The soldier passed the fire escape and pointed his flashlight down the alley. His steps were slow, but the heavy boots did not mask his gait as he continued further into the alley. As the soldier neared, Gallagher's head began to throb. *The headache*, he thought. The beginning of de-existence.

As the soldier neared his position, Gallagher believed his life was about to come to an end.

The soldier pointed the flashlight toward the alcove and called back to the other two soldiers, "*Hier!*"

As the other two hurriedly approached, the flashlight came fully into the doorway, illuminating the hidden Gallagher. One of the other soldiers addressed the soldier holding the flashlight, "*Ja, Korporal?*"

"*In der tür.*" The German corporal pointed to where Gallagher was hiding. The other two soldiers pulled their flashlights out and pointed the additional light into the alcove. "*Raus!*"

Gallagher raised his shaking hands as he stood up and stepped out of the alcove. He was squinting his left eye to fight off the pain of the engulfing headache. Time travel and interference with the past had consequences and came with the possibility of the ultimate price. Gallagher believed it was now time for him to pay.

The corporal was motioning with his flashlight to the center of the alley. Gallagher understood the soldier wanted him to come further out and stand in the bright lights of all the soldiers' flashlights. Slowly, Gallagher walked from the alcove into the center of the alley.

All three soldiers were now holding their flashlights on the sides of their rifles, pointing directly at Gallagher's chest. *There are too many guns being pointed at me today*, Gallagher thought as the pinching pain in his temple relaxed. The corporal asked what he was doing in the alley. "*Was machst du hier?*"

Gallagher remained still.

The soldier asked again but with a much stronger tone. Startled at the loud voice, Gallagher shrugged his shoulders. The headache was subsiding, and his thoughts were clearing. He gathered the energy and mumbled. "Fire?"

"*Was ist das?*" barked the soldier.

Gallagher slowly lowered his arms and spoke clearer in German. "*Feuer?*"

The soldier did not respond but waved his rifle in an up-and-down fashion. Gallagher knew to keep his arms well above his head. The soldier then motioned for the two additional soldiers to take Gallagher into custody. The soldiers lowered their rifles and approached as a fire truck was passing the alley on the street. The two soldiers stopped and turned to see the emergency vehicle heading to Müller's house.

The momentary distraction gave Gallagher his opportunity. When the soldiers turned their heads toward the street, Gallagher grabbed the end of the corporal's rifle and brought the muzzle down toward the ground. He then forcefully lifted the barrel of the rifle and rammed the buttstock upward into the corporal's nose, dazing him and causing his grip to loosen.

Gallagher pried the rifle from the corporal's hands and spun the soldier around, using his body as a shield. Holding the dazed corporal by his collar, he held up the rifle with one hand and pointed it at the other two soldiers. Gallagher motioned for them to put their rifles down. The soldiers lowered their rifles to their side. "*Runter!*" Gallagher insisted the weapons be placed on the ground. The soldiers knelt and placed their weapons on the ground.

Gallagher's human shield was still dazed and struggled to understand what was happening. Gallagher gripped the corporal tighter and walked around the two soldiers backward, heading to the entrance of the alley. He kept the rifle pointed toward the soldiers. One of the soldiers kneeled to pick up his rifle. Gallagher snapped, "*Nein!*" The soldier remained still as Gallagher opened the distance between him and the soldiers.

Gallagher's arms were beginning to throb from the weight of the rifle in one arm and holding the corporal, who was starting to struggle, in the other. Once clear of the alley and onto the street, Gallagher pushed the dazed corporal away, causing the soldier to lose his balance and nearly fall. Gallagher dropped the rifle and began running toward Müller's burning home. The two soldiers immediately began chasing Gallagher, passing the corporal as they neared the street.

Chapter 49
Trapped

The once-dark Berlin street was now glowing from the fire that raged through Müller's house. Firefighters were arriving to battle the fire while the soldiers were chasing Gallagher. As Gallagher ran down the street toward Müller's house, he positioned his body directly behind the fire truck, hoping the soldiers would not shoot, fearing they would miss and strike the emergency vehicle.

Reaching the fire truck, Gallagher ran on the far side of the truck from the blaze, passing the driver, who was jumping from the vehicle to begin battling the inferno. As he ran along the driver's side of the emergency vehicle, Gallagher bumped into the driver, nearly losing his balance. The firefighter yelled a word of frustration toward the intrusion but remained focused, moving to pull the hoses from the truck to fight the raging blaze.

As Gallagher regained his momentum, he turned back to see the two soldiers closing in on him. A few yards behind the soldiers, he also saw the corporal, who had regained his bearings and joined the pursuit. The light from the fire was a benefit to the soldiers. They were able to see their suspect running down the street as the glow illuminated the area around Müller's house. Moving past the fire truck, the two soldiers went to the left and the corporal to the right, allowing him to close the distance.

Gallagher reached the crossroads at the end of Müller's street. He crossed back over the street, closer to the buildings as he whirled right onto the side street. He remembered an alleyway that led to Müller's home. *There must be an entrance on the block.* Momentarily looking back, he did not see the soldiers yet turn the corner.

Running along the sidewalk as close to the buildings as possible, Gallagher scanned the structures for the entrance to the alleyway. Examining the row of adjoining buildings, he saw a gap between two of them. The concrete sidewalk had a break, and a brick drive went between the buildings, providing access to Müller's garage.

He could feel his lungs burn as he pushed hard to keep up his pace while he turned and ran down the alleyway toward Müller's garage. As he neared the carriage doors, the billowing smoke rising from the burning house was visible above the garage. Gallagher noticed the carriage doors were halfway open. At the end of the alleyway, the ladder was still resting against the wall that led to the neighboring building.

Gallagher leaned forward to accelerate his pace. He did not want to be shot climbing up the ladder. Reaching the ladder, he jumped to the third step and scaled up to the top. He grabbed the parapet of the neighboring building and kicked the ladder backward to make it fall to the ground. Lifting himself up onto the roof, he had successfully circled the block, moving toward the adjacent building. He just needed to jump over the parapet and make his way to the door overhang for the final climb to reach Foster and Brett.

Crossing the parapet onto the neighboring roof, Gallagher was immediately stopped in his tracks. Eva stood on the roof, pointing the muzzle of a familiar pistol in her steady hand. She had a fiery glow from the nearby flames, highlighting the rage in her eyes that echoed that of the devil. *There must have been a weapon in Müller's car*, Gallagher thought.

A sinister smile formed on Eva's face as the corner of her lips curled crookedly. She was about to pull the trigger when she heard the soldiers in the driveway resetting the ladder to climb onto the roof. Eva called to the soldiers, "*Hier oben! Der Amerikaner ist hier oben!*"

She then turned to Gallagher. "Only they will find you dead, American." Eva pointed the gun at his chest as he closed his eyes, just before she squeezed the trigger. A blast echoed in Gallagher's ears, and the Luger's bullet whizzed past his head, narrowly missing him. He opened his eyes to see her arms raised, pointing into the air as she recoiled backward.

Eva's body arched uncontrollably backward. Gallagher watched her crumple to the rooftop. From the shadows, a figure walked forward and into the fire's light. Standing above Eva's still body stood the colonel—*his* colonel from the PTE. She was holding and still pointing a stun gun, similar to the one brought aboard the *Titanic*.

"Time to go home, Mr. Gallagher," she simply said. "Please move next to me." Gallagher moved like an obedient child. The colonel pulled out a return pad and activated the console from the future. As the lasers opened the return cube, the first soldier climbed onto the roof. Gallagher could see it was the corporal.

The console in the future generated the power to open the time cube as the corporal approached, pointing the rifle at the colonel. Gallagher turned to the colonel, who was smiling. As the corporal began to shout, he stopped midsentence as a strobing cube formed and encapsulated Gallagher and the colonel. The hazy cube formed as the other two soldiers reached the rooftop. The three Nazi soldiers watched Gallagher and the colonel be encapsulated. Moments later, the cube disappeared along with the two suspects. Speechless, the corporal looked to the other two soldiers as they listened to the scorching crackle of the house burning nearby.

Chapter 50
Return Home

In the blink of an eye, Gallagher watched the dark rooftop with a soldier shouting and pointing a rifle at the colonel disappear and be replaced by the inside of the PTE cargo truck. The colonel stood next to him, still nodding with a hint of a smile. Turning, Gallagher saw Foster, Brett, and Maurice standing at the console. Foster still had the canvas bag around his shoulder, while next to him, Brett was struggling in pain.

"Welcome back," Foster said. He then turned to Brett. The bandage around the gunshot wound was soaked, and the pale color of Brett's face made it clear that he had lost a great deal of blood. "Brett didn't want to leave without making sure you made it back home. But now we should get him to the hospital."

The colonel walked off the portation pad, picked up a cell phone next to the console keyboard, and dialed a preset number. "Command Beta, we need a medic, QRF." She reached out her arm to Brett. "Can you walk?"

Brett nodded. "Yes, it's not that bad."

"Probably just a nick," she joked and pointed to the chairs by the wall. "Med is en route. Have a seat."

"Thank you, Colonel," Brett mumbled.

Gallagher stepped off the portation pad and walked up to the colonel. "Colonel, what …" He was lost for words.

"Are you asking me how I found you?"

"Um, yes. I … you could have, um …" He struggled with his thoughts as his mind raced through being saved from a bullet from Müller's niece.

The colonel interrupted his rambling. "Mr. Gallagher, you will have time to gather your thoughts. For now, the short answer is Dr. Foster and Mr. Brett returned and said you were being chased. There was little choice. Either I return or let you de-exist. I chose the former."

"You were lucky I kept a spare stun gun," Maurice piped in.

Gallagher turned to Maurice, who had a smirk on his face. He nodded. "Thank you, Maurice."

"Don't mention it."

Two med-techs arrived at the PTE cargo truck, one carrying a medical bag and the other pulling a gurney up the freight truck stairs. The two medics immediately moved to Brett's aid. Foster began assisting him onto the gurney.

Gallagher, having gathered his composure, remembered the map. "Colonel, in return for saving me … I have something for you." He reached into his coat and pulled out the rolled map from his inside pocket. The colonel looked at the map and said nothing. "This should lead you to the hidden storage center," Gallagher added.

The colonel took the map and unrolled a small portion to see the East Prussia overview. As she rolled the map back up, she looked to Gallagher. "Well done, Mr. Gallagher. And well done, Dr. Foster and Mr. Brett."

The medics were rolling Brett off the PTE truck on the gurney. "Wait, just a minute, please," he pleaded. The medics stopped at the doorway, and Brett halfheartedly leaned up from the gurney. "Foster, show her."

The colonel turned to Foster inquisitively.

"There's something else." Foster lifted the canvas bag off his shoulders. He placed the bag onto the table and slid the linen-wrapped jeweled *Rubáiyát* from inside. He held the book out to the colonel as though presenting a gift to a friend.

The colonel held the book and stared at the cloth.

"Go ahead," Brett called from the gurney. "Unwrap it."

Apprehensively, the colonel began removing the linen from the book. The cloth opened, revealing the *Rubáiyát*. The colonel gazed upon the magnificent beauty of the artifact. "My word," she said.

Unlike Müller, she lifted the book and opened the cover, revealing the hand-painted pages of the translated poetry. Awestruck at the exquisite and meticulous gilded pages, the colonel, rarely lost for words, was only able to repeat herself. "My word."

Epilogue
The Amber Room

The colonel stood outside a tent under a rainy Russian overcast. Her boots were covered in mud. Müller's map led her team to an uninhabited, densely forested area, located between St. Petersburg and Moscow. Near a tree-covered hill, the team found the dormant entranceway to the sealed cave that Müller had marked with a triangle on the map. For the past seventy-five years, the forest overgrowth devoured the road and sealed the entrance to the cave. The PTE crew spent an entire day cutting through the overgrown roots, trees, and weeds that blocked the metal door into the cave.

 Working in collaboration with the Russian government, the colonel arranged for the area to be cordoned off, even though no one lived within miles of the cave. The colonel and her team led the mission, while Russian officials supervised the excavation. After the PTE crew pruned and removed the overgrowth to the entrance, welders were brought in to open the two sealed metal doors.

 After several hours, the colonel was called forward. "We're ready, ma'am."

 The colonel walked across the muddy trail that led to the entrance. Four crew members, standing on each side of the double doors, pried the sealed entranceway open. Dirt fell from above as the doors slowly opened. Once there was enough room to allow entry, the colonel cautiously walked through the opening along with her excavation crew. With an abundance of flashlights, the colonel led her crew into the dark cave.

 Walking down a low-ceilinged entranceway, she reached an interior antechamber with a higher roof. On one wall, another set of double doors blocked the entrance to the storehouse. After an hour of welding, the PTE crew was able to open the locked doors, their flashlights illuminating a large storage room the size of a school gymnasium. The storage area was filled with crates, some of which were stacked atop others.

"Hand me a pry bar," the colonel ordered.

The colonel used the pry bar to open one of the wooden crates. A PTE crew member helped lift the cover of the crate. Inside, a blanket rested on top. The colonel pulled back the blanket and flashed her light into the crate. Inside, she saw the corner of an amber panel adorned with gold-leaf trim.

Author Bio
Terry Q. Ó Brien

For Terry Q. O'Brien, the seed to become an author was sown as early as high school when he began writing short stories which led to studying Creative Writing in college and, later, writing as an educator for thirty years. His writing journey brought him to write a historical science fiction time-travel adventure for young adults, *The Quest for the Lost Amber Room*, the debut installment in a series.

Terry is currently an adjunct faculty for Northeastern Illinois University. With a minor in filmmaking, when he isn't writing, Terry enjoys live theatre, where he performs, acts, and writes play adaptations from screenplays and books. His daughter, Ashley, is currently a student at the University of Iowa. Terry lives between Dublin, Ireland and Lake Villa, Illinois with his dog, a Shiba Inu named Bella, and his cat, an American Orange named Stanley.